INTO THE GLEN

By the same author:

The Dragon Tales Chronicles:

Book I	*Quest for a Cave*
Book II	*Quest for a Friend*
Book III	*Quest for Adventure*
Book IV	*The Runaway*
Book V	*Dragons in Snow*
Book VI	*The Dragons' Call*

INTO THE GLEN

by

Judy Hayman

First published in Great Britain by Practical Inspiration Publishing, 2018

ISBN 978-1-78860-068-2

For more information on the Dragon Tales books, email info@alisonjones.com.

This one is for Elise, and also for Kate.

LISA

1

'D'you *really* want to go? It'll be bloody cold in March up there!'

'Nearly April…'

'April, May – still bloody cold up there, trust me.'

'We'd be digging trenches through perma-frost!'

'Probably no wi-fi. Bad enough getting a signal most of the time.'

'Great country though. Really wild! Might still be snow and iced-over lochs. We'll need skis and skates and crampons.'

'There might be dragons.'

The last comment was almost lost in the hubbub of voices, but Lisa heard it. So far, she had not added her voice to the conversation round the pub table, though she was as keen as any of the group on the Archaeology Department's planned field trip to the Highlands at the beginning of the Easter break, and quite prepared to brave the cold. She looked across at the quiet boy who had made that unexpected remark. Apart from his name – Matthew

Pritchard – she knew nothing about him, except that he was reputed to be one of the cleverest on her course. But that single sentence had given her quite a shock. It hadn't sounded like a jokey addition to the swirl of banter, and nobody else had picked up the idea and developed it into a cheerful fantasy. They had moved on to the likelihood of spartan conditions in Highland Youth Hostels and bothies. She had a feeling that those of the group who hailed from the south of England would be in for a shock!

She kept one eye on Matthew as she debated the need for new hiking boots with a friend. Cassie, who came from London, always seemed to have plenty of money, but Lisa knew she'd have to find the extra from this term's budget. Fearing the necessity of buying a later round, she refused a second half-pint of lager from the boy sitting beside Matthew, who also refused, and pushed his seat back preparing to leave the pub. She wished she knew him well enough to leave with him, but that might lead to all sorts of complications. However, as she drained the last of her drink, there was a cry of 'Typical!' and a blue scarf was retrieved from under the table.

'Matt's,' said the retriever. 'Not likely to see him 'til Friday.'

'I'm off too,' Lisa got up. 'Essay to finish. He'll be heading for Pollock, won't he? I'll probably be able to catch him up.' She caught the scarf as it was tossed across the table and turned to leave, shaking her head as Cassie half-heartedly offered to leave with her.

It seemed very dark outside after the brightness of the Pear Tree pub, but at least it was dry, though very cold. Turning to go up the road towards the Pollock Halls, she spotted Matthew, head down against the wind, heading in the same direction. She broke into a run and caught him up as he paused, waiting to cross the main road.

'Matthew!' she called, and he swung round, surprised. 'You left your scarf in the pub.'

'Did I? Oh, you're right, that is mine! Thanks!' He took the scarf and wound it round his neck. 'Thought I felt chilly! Forgot I'd brought it. You heading back to Pollock too?'

'Yeah. Essay to finish,' said Lisa, wondering how to bring up the subject of dragons without sounding crazy.

'Me too.' They walked on in silence. Lisa tried again.

'Are you going to go on the field trip?'

'Yeah, sounds good. It'll be great to do some real archaeology, even if it's freezing. You?'

'Yes, definitely!' She hesitated, then decided to bite the bullet. 'Matt, back in the pub, when we were all talking about the field trip, you said 'There might be dragons.' What made you say that?'

There was a pause. Lisa held her breath. Then Matthew gave a laugh, slightly forced. 'No idea! I was probably thinking of those words you get on the blank bits of maps – you know – *Here be Dragons!* In fantasy books, that kind of thing. I used to read them a lot when I was a kid.'

'Me too. Dragons were always my favourite. Unicorns too, but dragons lasted longer. The Highlands sounds a perfect place for them.'

Matthew laughed again. 'We can keep a look-out when we're not heads-down in a trench. There should be lots of interesting wildlife. Hopefully eagles – I'm rather keen on bird-spotting. You're in Ewing House aren't you? I can swing round that way. I'm in Baird.'

At the main door to her Hall, Lisa thanked him for walking her home. 'Fair return for the scarf,' he said. 'See you tomorrow.'

Lisa headed upstairs to her room feeling slightly let down. She had a strong feeling that Matthew was hiding something; that perhaps he too had experienced that amazing encounter that was still so alive in her thoughts, and even her dreams, despite the passage of the years. She needed to talk to someone, and there was only one person who would understand. What a good thing she had, in fact, finished her essay, she thought as she sent a message, 'Hi. Facetime tonight?'

It was almost an hour before Finn's familiar face appeared on her screen, with the usual background of posters and books in his room. Like her, he was in his first year at University, but in Glasgow studying chemistry and living in a flat, not Halls like herself.

'Something the matter?' he asked, after routine greetings.

'No. Just something odd. You know I told you that we're going up to the Highlands with Archaeology for the field trip? Well, we were all in the pub discussing it when this guy, Matthew, suddenly said 'There might be dragons'! No one else noticed – there were several conversations going on at the same time, as usual. But I did. It was as if he'd read my mind because I'd been thinking the same thing! I walked back to Hall with him – just us – and asked him why he'd said it, and he talked about maps with 'Here be dragons' on them. But he hesitated, and then changed the subject, and I just have this feeling that he was hiding something. Finn, I think he's seen dragons too! I'm sure he has. I can feel it!'

'Would that be one of your famous *feelings*?'

'Don't laugh!'

'Wouldn't dare…'

'Punch!' It was their private Facetime code.

'Ow! Okay, so what are you proposing to do about it?'

'I don't know!'

'Confront the guy and demand the truth?'

'No, can't do that. If I get to know him better, I might.'

'He's not a Highlander himself, is he? Red-haired and rugged? I've heard they can be a bit fey, second sight and all that.'

'Your prejudices are showing! No, he's not. I think his accent's slightly Welsh, but I'm not too sure. I don't know him that well.'

Finn leaned forward and fixed her with as beady an eye as was possible via a screen. 'Single? Good looking? Fanciable?'

'Shut up, Finn! Nothing like that. It was the dragon comment that interested me, that's all.'

'Hmmm!'

Lisa decided to ignore this. 'It is weird, though. Ever since I heard where we're going for the dig I can't get Emily and the other dragons out of my mind. It's as if she's calling to me. She lived in the Highlands, remember? They were only down near us because of the snow.'

Finn hesitated, twiddling a biro between his fingers. 'The Highlands is a big place. Look at a map! Miles of brown and green. And blue, of course. Lots of lochs. I wouldn't get your hopes up!' Lisa's disappointment was clear to see, even through the blurriness of the screen. 'It was nearly six years ago,' he said more gently. 'We have no idea how long dragons live. We don't know that they're still alive, even.'

'Oh yes they are. I know!'

'That's what you *want* to think, Lisa. You can't be sure.'

'And we know nobody's found them,' Lisa went on, ignoring his scepticism. 'The discovery of dragons would have been reported and there'd have been pictures of them, even if they were corpses, or even skeletons. There's been nothing. I think they're still hiding out up there, living their secret lives. I suppose Emily's grown up now. And that baby that Megan and I rescued must be quite big too. You never saw her, did you? She was a gorgeous bright gold and Meg wanted to keep her! She hasn't forgotten about our dragons, has she? I've still got those lovely pictures she painted.'

'She doesn't say much about them. She's always been scared she'd give away the secret to the wrong people. Perhaps she's afraid of getting laughed at, too. You know what she's like.'

'Charlie hasn't mentioned them for years.'

'They don't have a football team. He gets more obsessed every time I see him. If you can't kick it…'

Lisa grinned. 'I know! All right, Finn, I promise I won't get too obsessed about our dragons. You're probably right, and I've far too many other things to think about. Thanks for listening. Gotta go!'

'Cheers 'til next time!' Finn smiled and clicked his computer off. He hoped that Lisa wouldn't spend the night spinning dreams of dragons. The two encounters with the exotic creatures was still one of the most vivid memories of his own early teens, but he was aware that to Lisa it was as if it had happened yesterday. She had memorised every detail, and he guessed she spent a lot of time secretly reliving the events. He was glad she still talked to him about it; it made a bond between them that he didn't want to break. But if she had hopes of finding Emily and her family again, he was sure she was doomed to disappointment.

When her screen went dark, Lisa didn't put the light on. Instead she sat staring out of the window at the looming bulk of Arthur's Seat, the main hill in Holyrood Park. When she had visited Edinburgh University's Open Day before she made the decision on where she would apply, the area of craggy hills near the centre of the city, with the University's Pollock Halls campus huddled right on the edge, had sold it to her. It was as far removed from an ordinary city park as it was possible to be, and the discovery that it was, in fact, the core of an ancient volcano just added to its romantic appeal. When she was allocated a high study-bedroom that looked straight out onto the hill, she was ecstatic. By day it was bright with gorse and alive with walkers, joggers and sight-seers, but at night it changed with the weather; hidden in mist, veiled in driving rain, lit and mysteriously shadowed in moonlight. Tonight, it was dark with a few stars visible in the strip of sky above the hill. 'There might be dragons…' she thought, smiling to herself. Then she almost jumped to her feet in astonishment. A tiny flame flickered briefly against the darkness of the hill. It was almost as if her thoughts had made it happen! Then she relaxed, grinning at herself. Obviously, someone out walking late had flicked a lighter. Better get to bed before she *really* started seeing things! She drew her curtains across before putting on the light.

2

After a night disturbed by muddled dreams, Lisa lay awake the next morning, reliving in her mind the three brief meetings with that colourful group of dragons that she remembered in such vivid detail. She and Finn, with Finn's young sister, Megan and her own brother Charlie had solemnly vowed to keep the existence of dragons a dead secret, and they had kept their promise. Finn, like herself, had understood their dread of discovery and the awful consequences that might follow. It didn't take much imagination to feel the horrors of a cage to creatures that could fly. Not creatures, she corrected herself silently, *people* - who might be covered in bright scales and sport wings and talons, but who could talk and think and make plans. They were *people*, who had friends and families like she had…

This was no good! She had to print out her essay before the 10 o'clock lecture, have a shower and hair-wash - and her long fair hair was so thick it took ages to dry…

She climbed out of bed.

After breakfast, she and Cassie, who lived two floors down, met to walk together to the lecture. They were bundled in thick coats, scarves and bobble hats, but still felt the bite of the wind as they left the Halls, skirted the Commonwealth Pool and headed for the main University buildings. There was something strange about the wind in Edinburgh, Lisa thought – whichever way you walked it was *always* blowing in your face. She had been told that it was because of the funnelling effect of hills and tall buildings, but she preferred to think of it as deliberate. 'It's the city's secret weapon against the English,' she had once said to Cassie, but her friend lacked her fanciful imagination, and she had learnt not to voice it too often. Not a person to confide her dragons to… She was doing it again! She must forget dragons and concentrate on real life… What was Cassie saying?

'Did you catch up with that guy Matt? Apparently, he's always leaving things behind. A right absent-minded Professor! Did he utter more than two words on the way home? Can't imagine it! Mind you, I quite fancy his friend, Rob. Pretty fit! Pity he's going out with Fiona. Probably won't last, though. Hers never do.' She turned to look more closely at Lisa. '*Did* he manage a conversation, or just grab his scarf and flee?'

Lisa laughed and tried for an off-hand tone. 'Yeah, we chatted a bit. He walked me to the door. He's OK on his own. He kind of disappears in a crowd, doesn't he?'

'Certainly does! Bit of a nerd if you ask me.' To Lisa's relief, Cassie seemed to consider the subject closed.

Unfortunately, however hard she tried, Lisa couldn't get Matthew's words out of her mind. In the lecture room, she saw his dark head three rows below, but there was no chance to speak to him, as he bundled his notes into his bag and departed as soon as the lecture was over, flashing her a brief smile as he passed, but not stopping. 'Forget it, forget it!' she thought, heading for the coffee bar with Cassie, who fortunately hadn't noticed the smile.

3

In the days that followed, Lisa did her best to concentrate on real life, and was reasonably successful. She was thoroughly enjoying the buzz of student life, fascinated by her ecology course and increasingly interested in the archaeology that was her subsidiary subject, and the reason for the field trip. She had signed up for it; so far, the only girl to do so, but determined not to be put off by that. She had tried to think of a way to speak to Matthew again, and failed to come up with a convincing one. Perhaps if Cassie succeeded in her determined pursuit of his friend Rob they might get a chance to meet up as a four? 'And what good would that be?' she asked herself. 'Just embarrassing! Forget it! Forget the whole thing!'

She had succeeded in putting Matthew – and dragons - to the back of her mind when there was an unexpected development three weeks later. She was sitting over coffee with Cassie and a few others from her course, including Rob (still uncaptured, despite Cassie's best efforts) when Matthew burst through the door and joined them. He was unusually animated – not to say distraught.

'My bloody computer! I know it's pretty elderly, but why did it choose *today* to pack in? I'd just started that essay for Dr Andrews, and it swallowed all his lecture notes! And mine! I've left it a bit late as well. What the hell am I going to do? Oh, thanks!' He glanced up at Rob, who, seeing his state, had brought him a coffee, and took a desperate swig.

Lisa leaned forward across the table. 'I took a print-out of Dr A's notes. I always work better from paper. D'you want a copy?'

Matthew almost choked on his coffee. 'Really! Could I? You are a life-saver! Have you finished with them?'

'No, but I can print another copy. Can't do much about your own notes though.' She thought quickly, avoiding the beady eye that Cassie was casting over her. Wednesday; Cassie's choir rehearsal night. 'I'll be in tonight if you want to come and collect them,' she said, getting up. 'Room 306 in Ewing. Need to get to the library. See you later then?'

'Sure – life-saver, like I said! 306, right!'

Lisa smiled and departed. Never mind real life – time to give fantasy a go! She would ponder her approach on the way home.

That evening she tried in vain to concentrate on a book from her reading list and hoped Matthew wouldn't be too late. The last thing she wanted was for him to snatch up the notes and rush away. Fortunately, it was around eight when she heard a knock on her door and Matthew appeared.

'Sorry to disturb you if you're working,' he said, hovering by the door.

'It's fine, come in. Kettle's hot – sit down and I'll make us a coffee.' As she got up, Matthew moved across to the window, un-curtained as usual, and looked out at the hill, lit tonight by a three-quarter moon.

'Wow, you are SO lucky!' he said, peering beyond his own reflection. 'A view of Arthur's Seat! I look over the courtyard to the Hall over the way. And I'm first floor, so it's noisy too. How did you swing this? Have you got secret connections?'

'Just luck! But you're right, it's great and I love it, 'specially at night. Milk? Sugar?'

'Just milk. Thanks.'

Lisa passed the coffee, opened a new packet of Jaffa-cakes, sat down on the bed and took a deep breath. 'Bite the bullet!' she told herself. 'I saw a dragon once,' she remarked casually, as if they were in the middle of a conversation. 'In fact, several dragons, several times. It was a few years ago, just near my home in the depths of Northumberland. It was that very snowy winter, remember? There was a whole group of them living in the ruins of an old mansion house. Actually, there was quite a lot of the house intact, but it was fenced off because of the danger it might collapse. Me and my brother and two friends went in to explore, through a hole in the wire. The young dragons were in the old cellars; it was rather cosy, they had beds of hay and straw. We got quite friendly and they told us lots about themselves…' She paused, glancing at his expression. 'I'm not mad, and I'm *not* making this up,' she continued. 'I never talk about it, but I'm telling *you* because I *think*, from something you said in the pub the other week, that you've seen one too. Have you?'

Matthew was looking utterly flabbergasted, almost panic-stricken. 'Are you saying you *talked* to the dragons? They can *speak*?'

'Oh yes, just as well as we can. They're very intelligent. Tell me about yours.'

Matthew swallowed hard. 'I've never told anyone before…' he started.

'That's all right, I can keep secrets. I've been keeping this one for years!'

He took a deep breath and gazed into the coffee mug cradled in his hands. 'It was one day in the spring six years ago, on the Welsh coast just south of the Lleyn peninsula. I was with my uncle and his partner, in their hot-air balloon.'

'Wow!' said Lisa, under her breath.

'Yeah! It was the first time he'd taken me up – he was only getting used to flying it himself. It was amazing – early morning, the sun just coming up – fantastic view of the country below and the line of the cliffs. Then the wind veered unexpectedly, and we started moving out towards the sea. That was a bit scary! We had a following jeep, like you always do, but that wouldn't be much help if we ditched in the bay. I could tell Uncle Geoff was a bit worried. But then suddenly we cleared the edge of a steep cliff, and there was a tiny cove below us, and at the edge of the water there were five dragons. We were flying quite low so we could see them clearly, and then they saw us – and you know what? They stood up and *waved*!' For the first time he looked directly at Lisa. She nodded.

'They're very brave,' she said, 'but you must have worried them. The only thing that scares them is being found by us – humans, that is.'

'There's something else,' Matthew continued, almost as though she had not spoken. 'Floating on the sea was a raft, with the body of a dragon lying on it, and we had spotted them breathing flames to set it alight and pushing it out on the sea as we cleared the cliff. It was just like a Viking burial ship! It floated below the balloon basket, and when we looked for it again, it had vanished. And as we drifted further away, we saw the others go up the beach to a little fire they had burning under the cliff. Then we lost sight of them among the boulders.'

Lisa was on the verge of tears. She could picture it so clearly. 'I wonder who had died,' she said quietly, almost to herself. Then she looked up. 'Must have been *fantastic*!' she said. 'And you never saw them again?'

Matthew took a swig of his cooling coffee. 'Actually, we did!' he continued. 'As the dragons disappeared, we got a radio call from the jeep. They'd seen us heading out to sea and directed Geoff and Greg to steer towards the northern headland, find a place to land and they'd pick us up. We'd kind of forgotten the danger we were in. They managed a bumpy landing, and when we'd recovered, pretty relieved, we agreed to say nothing about dragons to anyone. The guys in the jeep would have fallen about laughing! But much later, towards evening, the three of us walked out to the top of the cliff with binoculars, just to see if we could spot the dragons again. The whole thing felt a bit dream-like by then. But we saw them! We lay down on the edge of the cliff, and saw two of the dragons fly away westwards, over the sea, and then the rest took off too and headed north. It seemed to be quite an emotional farewell, somehow. Amazing, the whole day! I've never forgotten it.'

'I know! And none of you ever told anyone else about it?'

'No. Greg would have liked to take a photo, but Uncle Geoff said no. He said they seemed almost like people, and we should respect them and let them go.' His voice choked slightly, and he bent his head and took a deep breath. 'And…and two days later, he and Greg took the balloon up again, but this time they didn't come back. There was an accident. The balloon hit a power line and they were both killed.' Lisa gazed at him, horrified, but he didn't look up. 'It was awful. At least they were together – they'd been partners for years – but I missed them a lot.

Still do, when I'm home.' He drew in a deep breath and looked up as if remembering Lisa was there. 'It sounds stupid, but I felt that it was sort of Fate – the weirdness of seeing those creatures, and then the shock of the accident. I felt I should have been with them, so there could be no danger of anyone else finding out. I've tried to forget about them, but it keeps haunting me.'

'Me too,' said Lisa, trying to control a choke in her voice.

Matthew sniffed, blinked hard and tried to smile. 'Sorry,' he said. 'I've never talked about this before – not the dragons bit. It was a kind of vow I made to Geoff and Greg. Now I suppose I've broken it.'

Lisa shook her head. 'No, you haven't. I don't count. I've made the same vow. And I was lucky – I had someone else to talk to about it. 'Specially my friend Finn. And his sister, Megan, who was with us too. Did you ever see them again?'

'No. We watched them fly away, and that was the last we saw of them.' He turned away and stared at the dark bulk of Arthur's Seat beyond the window.

'One more thing,' Lisa said, after a pause. 'What colour were they?'

Matthew looked back at her, puzzled. 'I'm not sure. I think we were too stunned to take in details like that when we spotted them on the beach. In the evening, through the binoculars, it was better, but the light was fading. They were fairly well camouflaged into the background. Except for one. It was a very dark red, I remember.' Lisa held her breath. 'The others were greyish, greenish… blueish perhaps? Different colours anyway. We all noticed that. The biggest one seemed to have sort of painted bits of different colours, I think. You could see coloured stripes when it spread its wings'

'*His* wings. They're *people*!'

'Sorry! You don't think they were the *same* dragons, surely? This was in Wales!'

'Dragons can fly, remember! And yes, I'm pretty sure they were. Two of them anyway. Wow! This is *fantastic!* I wonder if Emily was one of them. She might have been, if one was blueish… '

Matthew watched her lapse into old memories, a wistful smile on her face. Suddenly the buzz of an incoming message on her phone made them both jump.

'I'd better go,' said Matthew, getting up. 'This has been a bit of a mind-blowing evening. Sorry! I feel shattered!' He got up and moved to the door.

'Matthew … don't forget the notes! That's what you came for.'

'Good point, thanks!' said Matthew, taking them. 'I've still got the wretched essay to finish before I can get to bed. Can't say I feel like getting back to it now!'

'Sorry – that's my fault! Bombarding you with dragons! There's lots more I could tell you, but we might need another cover story.'

'That'd be good. Thanks for the coffee.' He hesitated at the door, then smiled, reminiscently. 'You know, we thought of them as people too. That's what Geoff said. So, when they waved, we waved back!'

4

The term continued, full of work, lectures and social events. Lisa revelled in all of it. Although she saw him in lectures and sometimes round the table in the cafeteria, there was no chance of more dragon talk with Matthew for several weeks. She wanted to be careful not to start any rumours of a relationship between them. Groups of friends were still shifting, relationships forming and breaking and gossip was rife. Also, there were new interests to explore. Cassie persuaded Lisa to join her choir for their Easter concert. She had done a good deal of choral singing, and found that her high soprano, not powerful but very sweet and true, was welcomed with delight by the conductor. She had a feeling that she would not be allowed to leave the choir after the concert, and hoped that Cassie, whose voice she quickly outclassed, would not be bitchy about it. She was inclined to resent any rivalry. On the whole, though, the choir members formed a relaxed and sociable group, and it was nice meeting people from other years and different departments in the University.

At the end of February there was a heavy fall of snow, and sledging, snowboarding and skiing took up a good part of a week, causing late-night panic to complete essay deadlines. Finn came over on the train from Glasgow for the weekend, and joined them on the slopes, complaining that it had quickly turned to slush in the west, and making Lisa feel smug that she had chosen to study in Edinburgh. He was also envious of the view from her room; although he had rolled his eyes and sighed heavily when she told him it made her think of their dragons, she knew he secretly understood.

'Have you talked Dragon to that guy Matt again?' he asked, as they ate a pasta supper in her room. Matthew had joined them on the slopes during the morning, so Lisa had introduced them, briefly.

'No. It's tricky getting him on his own without risking the rumour mill. You know what it's like!'

'I certainly know what Cassie's like! What a flirt!'

'I'd like to tell him more. I heard his story, but there wasn't time to tell ours. And I haven't had another chance.'

'OK, so what you need is a chaperone. And here I am! I knew I'd be useful for something. Why don't you text and invite him over? Even better, why don't we take torches and have a walk up that hill? Perfect for secret talks about dragons!'

'You're mad! We'll freeze!'

'We'll be fine. Waterproofs have dried out, nearly. Come on! I want to see the place by moonlight.'

'The city lights *are* pretty amazing from up there,' Lisa admitted. 'OK, I'll see if he'll come.'

Slightly to her surprise, Matthew seemed perfectly happy to don damp boots and ski gear and meet them outside their Hall. Unbelievably there was no wind, the sky was clear and starry with a three-quarter moon, and even as they left the street lights behind, they could see the track clearly. It was a well-trodden path towards the top of Samson's Ribs, the line of sheer cliffs that ran below the summit; an ancient land-slip, the day-time haunt of rock-climbers and geologists. At the top they found a flat rock, swept clear of snow by previous climbers, and sat in a row, getting their breath back and gazing down at the lights of the city below. They had seen no one on the way up.

'Nobody else mad enough,' Matthew remarked.

'No other closet dragon-buddies,' said Finn. 'I'm another one, you know. No quite as obsessed as Lisa, but part of the same secret society. Welcome aboard!'

'Did you tell him?' Matthew turned to Lisa. It was almost an accusation.

'Just about your sighting of our dragons,' Lisa was defensive. She had not, in fact, told Finn the more personal details of Matthew's story, the tragic loss of his uncle and partner. 'We're sure they *were* ours. The one with painted bits was obviously Des, the one who scared us to a jelly when we first met in the cellar. So the red one was probably Ollie.'

'We weren't *that* scared!' Finn said defensively.

'Yes, we were! Charlie even grabbed my hand – and he NEVER did that, even then. He's my brother,' she added for Matthew's benefit. 'He was quite wee then, but now he's taller than me, football mad and so macho that he's put dragons and all things magical right out of his head.'

'I can't believe they have *names*,' said Matthew. 'Are you sure you haven't invented that?'

'No, honestly! We all sat down together in their cellar and introduced ourselves. At least, three of them did – Ollie was a lot more suspicious. There was Emily and her younger brother Tom, who were blue dragons, from Scotland, and Alice, Ollie's sister, who was red, but not as dark as Ollie. And apparently, upstairs in the old house, there were lots more; the grown-ups. The only big one we saw was Des. We really didn't want to meet the rest – he was scary enough!'

'Ollie was desperate to get us out of there,' Finn continued. 'He took me outside to work out how to get us away without their grown-ups finding out. He mentioned that he had once been captured and caged back in Scotland, which was why he hated humans. We never found out why that didn't hit the headlines. You'd think *Dragons are real after all!!* would have sparked some interest.'

'Once Ollie was out of the way the rest of us got quite friendly,' said Lisa. 'We got on really well with Emily and Alice. We found out they could read as well.'

'Now you ARE having me on!'

'No, honestly! We passed over some of our old books, and they were delighted. Oh, I wish I knew where they are now! I'd give *anything* to see them again.'

She sounded so forlorn that Finn put an arm round her and gave a sympathetic hug. 'I'm freezing. Let's head back down. This is where I miss the Christmas markets. I could just do with a tumbler of that lovely hot German gluhwein.'

Lisa let him pull her to her feet. 'Hot chocolate would be nearly as good,' she said. 'We could go to the café on the corner. Come on! Watch your feet – it'll be slippy going down."

'I'll head back,' Matthew said, slightly awkwardly, when they reached the bottom of the path safely and could walk abreast again.

'Oh no, come for hot chocolate!' Lisa insisted. 'We've lots more to tell you. It's all right – we're not a couple or anything – just best mates from way back,' she added. Matthew agreed to join them, but glancing at the expression on Finn's face, he was not at all sure that he felt the same way. He decided he'd better tread carefully.

The café was quiet and the three of them were able to huddle around a corner table, warming frozen hands round their steaming mugs.

'Was that the only time you saw them?' Matthew resumed the conversation quietly, carefully avoiding the 'dragon' word in case they were overheard by the other four occupants of the café. 'I presume you didn't ever see the big ones, or you'd have been charred to a crisp.' The tone of his voice told both Finn and Lisa that he was still finding it hard to *entirely* believe the story they were telling.

'Actually, we spotted them again about three weeks later, quite by chance,' said Finn. 'The snow had just about melted, and we were back at school, but one horrible wet Sunday the two of us took Lisa's Labradors for a walk and came upon all five of them. They were diving and swimming in a pond not far away, on the edge of the woods where the old house was. The dogs were terrified! We only had time for a very brief chat, and they said they were leaving soon. We promised again to say nothing to anyone. The big one, Des, was still pretty suspicious. That was the last I ever saw of them.'

'But I met two of them again just a couple of days later.' Lisa lowered her voice as a few other people came through the café door, and the boys leaned in. 'This time it was Megan and me out with the dogs in the woods. We heard them barking madly up ahead, and when we reached them, we found a little gold dragon clinging to the branch of a tree. She jumped down to Megan, and we carried her home, shut the dogs in and then headed back towards the old house. We guessed the others would be looking for her, and we hadn't gone far before we found Alice and Ollie, and they took her home with them. By then, they said, Emily and the rest of her family had headed back home to Scotland. Megan hated giving the wee one back, but it made up for missing the meeting by the pond. She was furious when we told her about that!'

'And you've no photos to prove any of this?'

'No. I would have loved to take just one, but we all agreed it was too risky. You could *feel* their terror of discovery. We couldn't bear to make it worse for them. I've got something nearly as good, though.' She fished out her phone, brought up a series of pictures, and handed it to Matthew.

'I never realised you'd photographed them!' Finn exclaimed, looking over Matthew's shoulder. 'That's a neat idea, and safe too! My sister Megan painted them from memory, a couple of years later,' he explained. 'She's turning into a pretty good artist, especially of birds and beasts. She did those for Lisa's birthday. And obviously, as far as anyone else was concerned, they came straight out of her imagination!'

'I'll show you the originals one day,' Lisa promised, taking her phone back. 'They are the same as the dragons you saw, aren't they?'

'Yes, I think so. I'm pretty sure of the painted one. But we can't be the only people who've seen them, surely,' Matthew went on, thoughtfully. 'Won't other people have explored that old house of yours? Perhaps there are dozens of people like us, knowing they exist, but keeping quiet about it!'

'The fence was high and festooned with warning notices, and the old house was finally demolished four years ago,' said Finn. 'We presumed if any of them were still living there, they fled before the bulldozers moved in. There were certainly no reports of any strange sightings – we kept checking in the local rag. So that would seem to be the end of it. Just a memory!'

Matthew glanced across at Lisa and saw her brows come together in a scowl. 'You don't want to believe that, right?' he said.

'Of course I don't!'

'She gets these *'feelings'*,' said Finn, and dodged before the punch was delivered.

'I have high hopes of the Highlands!' Lisa said loftily, ignoring him and addressing Matthew. 'While we're there, we might get the chance to do a bit of exploring and searching on our own. I'm sure we'll get the odd chance to skive off the dig. You'll come and search with me, won't you, Matt?'

'Sure! I'm known as a birdwatcher, so we can pretend it's eagles I'm looking for.'

It was Finn's turn to scowl.

Soon after that, the café filled up and the three of them headed back to the Halls, Matthew to his room in Baird and Finn to roll into his sleeping bag on the floor of Lisa's room. She lent him her yoga mat and a couple of cushions.

'That was really good,' she said when they had put the light out and were settling down to sleep. 'I'm glad you had the idea of going up the hill in the dark.'

'Seems a nice guy, that Matthew,' said Finn.

'Yes, I like him too.'

There was a pause. 'Sure you don't fancy him as well?'

Lisa propped herself on one elbow and glared at the humped shape of Finn on the floor. 'No! I said I *like* him. You sound like Cassie! She's always assuming things like that – it drives me mad. If you're going to start getting jealous, I won't ask you to come again. '*Best mates from way back*' remember? We agreed, before we left for uni in the summer.'

'*You* did!' Finn muttered to himself, but aloud he said. 'Yeah, yeah, whatever you say. Best mates and dragon-buddies! Night, Lisa!'

5

Not everyone from the first-year archaeology course had opted for the Highland field trip at the beginning of April. Cassie was not one of the group. She had given up her pursuit of Rob and was now going out with a third-year tenor from the choir. 'Enjoy yourself with Professor Ma-att!' she sang, giving Lisa a hug before departing for the station and her London home. 'I will!' said Lisa, but only to herself, as she waved her away.

The mini bus, with eight first-year students, two post-grads and Dr Andrews driving, was laden with camping gear, bulging rucksacks and all the bulky equipment necessary for a dig. They had studied aerial photos of the site, which was thought to show the remains of an early mediaeval castle on a craggy outcrop, of which very little remained on the surface. Geophysical surveys, taken a couple of years before, had revealed the possibility of a much earlier settlement to the south of the castle, and they were joining a group from Aberdeen University, who had started the dig two weeks earlier. They had been given a bare three weeks to conduct the excavation by the local Factor, acting on behalf of the landowner, a Middle Eastern minor royal whose only interest in the large tract of land he had purchased was one annual grouse shoot, attended by the rich and famous.

Lisa was sitting next to the only other girl, a PhD student called Sophie, and listening with interest to her stories of past digs as the mini-bus rattled northwards. 'My first-year trip was just to the Borders,' Sophie said. 'In a field near Melrose. We were hoping for another Roman site, like Trimontium, but we didn't find a thing. And it rained all week!'

'It obviously didn't put you off,' said Lisa.

'No, digs are always good fun,' Sophie replied. 'This one sounds promising. The Aberdeen lot have already made a few finds. It's not likely to be as good as my best one though. That was in Orkney. It looked like a bare hillside, but honestly, under the surface turf we seemed to scoop an artefact every few minutes.'

'I've never been to Orkney,' Lisa confessed.

'Oh, you must! It's amazing! Pre-history wherever you look. I'm going to spend the summer at the new Ness of Brodgar dig. That's *really* big.'

'I've seen a programme about it on TV.'

'Yes, it *has* hit the headlines. The sightseers and tourists are a pain, but at least all the publicity has brought in the funding. This site won't be anything like that. It's pretty remote – no roads anywhere near, and not even decent tracks. We'll leave the bus at an old hostel. Doc Dave's arranged to borrow an ancient jeep for the gear, but the rest of us will have to trek over. Hence the tents. We'll camp beside the site, and just hope it doesn't snow.'

'There's still some up there,' Lisa pointed out of the window to the sunlit hills, becoming more rugged and more like proper mountains with every mile. She felt excitement rise. Beside her, Sophie had fished mints out of her bag and was passing them round the bus. She turned, caught Matthew's eye, and a conspiratorial grin passed between them.

Not long after a welcome stop for late lunch and loo break at a roadside café, backed by woodland and with scattered wooden picnic tables waiting for the tourists of summer, they turned off the main road and headed towards the mountains. This road was narrow and winding, with passing places, but they met no other traffic save for one tractor early on and then an ancient Land Rover so covered in mud it resembled a moving mound of earth. Their way rose steadily, the road surface deteriorated and the snowline came nearer.

'It looks as though we might need skis after all!' she heard Matthew say, behind her, but the other post-grad, Harry, was reassuring.

'There isn't any at the height of the dig,' he said. 'At least there wasn't a couple of days ago, when I last heard. They've dug the first trenches, so the ground can't be frozen hard. Difficult to get news – needless to say, there's no signal on site. There's a radio at the camp, but only in case of an emergency, not for routine gossip.'

'We're about fifteen miles from the hostel,' the driver called back over the pounding rock bands that had replaced Radio 1 at the insistence of the boys at the back. 'Everyone OK to press on? It'll get bumpier from now on!' There was a cheerful chorus of assent.

'I can't believe nobody's been travel-sick,' Sophie remarked. 'There's nearly always one!' Lisa, who *had* been starting to feel a bit queasy, swallowed hard and sucked another mint. 'Look, deer!' Sophie pointed, and the excitement of a close view of a small herd of red deer was enough to remove the threat from Lisa's mind. A particularly majestic stag stood in the road, and they had to pull up and wait for him to leap the ditch and follow his hinds across the tussocky moor. 'Fair enough. His patch!' said Matthew. It was as good as a safari park, Lisa thought, as grouse scuttled across the road in front of them, then a mountain hare, still wearing winter white; a curlew on a tree-stump looked as if it might over-balance onto its own long slender bill, and a buzzard circled lazily high overhead. Every lurching corner brought new views of black crags and white peaks. Near the main road, they had passed a couple of isolated farms and the occasional imposing stone house, set in trees and guarded by walls and iron gates, but for miles there had been no sign of human habitation, except the dilapidated remnants of dry-stone walls.

Eventually, they rounded a sharp bend and descended sharply. The road became even more stony and rutted, and ahead they saw a narrow valley with a small river widening into a reedy loch, and a weather-beaten building with tiny windows and a mossy roof set back from the track. 'Here we are!' said Dave Andrews. 'Made it before dark, thank goodness! Welcome to the least luxurious accommodation in the Highlands. It's usually closed, but we got permission to open it up for the three weeks' dig. It's basic, but there is running water and a generator for electricity. When it works! This part of the Highlands isn't on the main trekking routes, so it's the best we can do.'

Lisa climbed stiffly down from the bus and joined the rest in unloading their gear. A freezing wind was funnelling down the valley, and they all zipped anoraks and pulled on hats and gloves. Then, under Dave's direction, everyone helped to empty the bus of stores of food and the equipment needed at the dig and load it straight into the back of the battered Land Rover that was parked at the front door. There was barely room for a driver once that was done.

'No point trekking up there tonight,' Dave assured the group. 'There's a hot supper waiting for us, so we'll spend the night here and head up first thing tomorrow. Accommodation's pretty basic, but it'll be warmer than tents for the rest of the week, so make the most of it. The site's seven miles up the glen, and quite a scramble in places. It looks as though you've all brought far too much! I suggest you check your bags and leave behind all but the absolute essentials for the six days. We're the only people using this place, so it'll be quite safe. Full waterproofs necessary, of course, plenty of sweaters and all your spare socks, but nobody needs to change for dinner! The week's forecast isn't too bad, fortunately, but you can never be sure, up here.'

There was a scramble to collect rucksacks, and they all surged through the front door into a steamy smell of cooking chilli. Dave introduced the cooks – Tim and Nancy, from Aberdeen – and stayed in the kitchen to hear news of the dig's progress, while Sophie and Harry led the group up rickety stairs to two low-ceilinged dormitories. Lisa felt quite sorry for the boys, crammed into the larger one, while she and Sophie had plenty of space in a room to themselves. 'Choose your bunk,' said Sophie. 'Top or bottom, whichever you prefer! I'd keep away from the window – there's bound to be a draught. There's a very basic shower and loo next door, and another across the passage. I suppose we'd better share with the lads. Hardly fair to have one for just us, while they're queuing down the stairs. You OK with that?'

'Sure!' said Lisa cheerfully. 'Think I'll go now, before the queue forms.' She disappeared, and Sophie smiled to herself. Obviously, this girl was going to cope with roughing it for a week. Good thing that friend of hers had changed her mind about the trip, though, she thought; definitely *not* the type to enjoy mud, camp food and the lack of a hair-straightener!

Later, over steaming bowls of chilli with rice, they heard what progress had been made on the dig so far, and then, when the supper had been cleared, pored over large scale Ordinance Survey maps spread out on the table. It really was amazingly empty country, Lisa thought, noting that a river ran through the valley where the dig site was, and there was a tiny lochan close by. A stream ran steeply down a glen running up into the higher hills at right angles to the main valley and joined the river. The whole area was enclosed by rugged mountains and empty tracts of moorland.

'That's the track we take with the Land Rover,' Dave Andrews traced the line. 'You walkers can follow it too, though you can save nearly a mile by cutting across *here*. It's boggy in places, but not too bad. I'm taking one passenger. Sandy.'

Sandy, a rugby-playing Borderer and the largest of the students, looked a bit abashed at this, and directed an apologetic glance at Lisa. 'Several reasons,' Dave continued, 'he'll be the strongest for pushing the jeep out of trouble, which is bound to happen, he has a driving licence, in case we need to take turns to push, and he's used to driving over rough terrain.'

'I grew up on a hill farm in the Borders,' Sandy explained. 'Sorry, Doc Dave's decision, not mine, honestly! I could nurse some extra luggage if that helps.'

'OK, any questions?'

'Is there *any* chance of a signal up here?' asked one of the boys, Phil, plaintively.

'Very little! But you can try, if you like. It's always handy for texts. In my experience, it fades out just as you type the last word. No internet, obviously! You'll survive.' Phil and a couple of other students looked doubtful.

He fielded a few more questions about the dig, and the practicalities of the week, then urged them all to an early night. 'Breakfast at 6.30, so that we can start as soon as it's properly light. No lingering in the shower. You won't want to anyway, trust me! Sort your packs tonight. Keep your torches handy – the generator goes off at eleven. Sleep well – I can guarantee there won't be any traffic noise!'

'But don't panic if you hear a loud roaring,' Harry added. 'It'll be a stag, not a bear or a wolf or a mythical monster. Sorry to disappoint!' Lisa caught Matthew's eye and he gave the ghost of a wink.

Upstairs, she got ready for bed and waited for Sophie to finish in the bathroom. Her pack was ready, with tomorrow's clothes laid out on the upper bunk to save time in the morning. It was completely dark outside, no moon or stars shining, and no sign of a light anywhere. She gave a shiver of excitement and climbed happily into bed. Perfect wild and empty country, she thought to herself – '*Here be dragons*' – I wish!

6

She was awake before the alarm call next morning, after a restless night on a lumpy mattress, so was able to get through the shower before the rush and had time to plait her hair before breakfast. It could stay like that all week, easily pinned up out of the way when necessary. By the time everyone was down, and fed, additional spades and pick-axes had been strapped on the roof of the laden Land Rover. 'Think you might need to be the passenger after all, Lisa,' Sandy remarked. 'My weight could be the last straw.' However, Dave insisted on his original plan, and the rest of the group watched the battered vehicle jolt over the ruts of the drive and head up the track. It disappeared round the bend in a cloud of exhaust.

'Makes me feel guilty, polluting this pristine air!' Sophie said critically as the rest of the party shouldered their packs, checked the laces on their boots and prepared to set off. 'Let's not follow too closely.'

They started to climb almost immediately, and conversation died away as the gradient increased. Harry and Sophie set a steady pace, and Lisa was glad she had done some training on Arthur's Seat during the term. She had an irrational fear of being unable to keep up with the rest of the group, but in fact she found that she wasn't the slowest. The Land Rover was out of sight round the curve of the hillside.

After three miles, they reached the point where the 'short cut' left the main track. Sophie checked the map, and they all agreed to try it. The ground was still firm with frost, so boggy patches would be less of a hazard, they reasoned. But as they were heading off, a yell from behind made them stop and turn round. Sandy was standing further back along the track gesturing for help. 'Jeep's stuck!' he yelled up to them.

Harry sighed. 'Typical! Better go and help push. Come on!'

They headed back to the track and at the top of the rise looked down on the Land Rover with its wheels hopelessly stuck in a patch of mud. Dave was using one of the spades to try to clear a path.

'The sun's got to that bit and melted the frost,' Sandy explained as they headed towards it. 'We tried to push in turns, but it was no good. Needs more of us.'

'And perhaps some half-decent tyres?' suggested Paul, the only one of the party who had cast a critical gaze on their elderly vehicle the evening before.

'Yes, all right, I know it's past its first youth,' said Dave. 'Sophie, you get behind the wheel and I'll help to push. Don't rev too hard.'

'I know!' said Sophie, climbing in. 'Not my first stuck truck! Lisa, stand well back, or you'll get splattered.'

Eight boots dug firmly into the mud and four shoulders heaved and slowly the Land Rover lurched out of the hole the tyres had dug and staggered up the track. Sophie, revving hard as soon as she was clear, drove further up.

'Hey, stop!' Paul shouted.

'She's heading for the top of the rise,' Dave said, shouldering her pack, and was proved right, as Sophie stopped at the top of the slope and climbed out. The others joined her. It was obvious that they would have to abandon the idea of the short cut.

'You should be all right from now on,' she said.

'Not sure,' said Dave, shielding his eyes as he peered along the track. 'Looks like another bad bit just before the bend.'

'That one shouldn't be a problem!' Sophie said, with the hint of a challenge in her voice.

'OK, on you go!' said Dave. 'I'll walk for a bit. We'll be along in a few minutes to push you out.'

'Right, you're on!' said Sophie. 'Come on, Lisa, hop in. Sandy's pack's in here, but he can take yours.'

Lisa handed it over. 'Sorry!' she said, but Sandy laughed. '*You* might be sorry in two minutes,' he said. 'Springs have gone. It's really bad on the backside!'

Lisa saw what he meant, as Sophie careered down the slope, heading for the mud patch. She braced herself for the jolt or skid, but Sophie cleverly swung the jeep sideways onto the bank, where it hung at an angle, but kept going. Lisa shut her eyes until she felt it level out.

'There!' said Sophie. 'Piece of cake! Honestly, *blokes*! They always think they know best when it comes to vehicles. May as well keep going, don't you think?'

'You're the boss,' said Lisa, grinning. 'I'm just along for the ride.' She put her feet on Sandy's pack in the well and peered ahead through the spattered windscreen. 'Track looks a bit better up ahead.'

'Cross your fingers then. No guarantee I'll be able to get through the next bad bit. We really don't want to have to wait for a push. I'd never hear the last of it all week!'

By the time they came in sight of the castle mound, with the dig settlement at its feet, Lisa was heartily agreeing with Sandy about the effect of bumps on the backside, but she cheered with Sophie as they drove up to the line of tents with a flourish, parked and climbed out.

By the time the rest of the party arrived, they had pitched Sophie's tent, staked out a pitch for Lisa when her pack arrived, been introduced to the Aberdeen group and inspected the progress of the dig in the neat parallel trenches. The spades and picks had been commandeered and a new trench started where markers had been laid out. 'It follows the hints from the geophys survey,' Sophie explained. 'But it's mainly luck. We might strike something interesting, we might not!'

Lisa went across to reclaim her pack from Sandy. 'Good to see you're still alive!' he said, handing it over. 'That Sophie's a hell of a driver! How's the bum?'

'Sore. How are the legs?'

'His might be OK, but my knees are creaking,' Matthew said, joining them. 'We were terrified watching you on that mud patch,' he added. 'The jeep looked as though it would overbalance any minute. Doc Dave just covered his eyes and swore. Not sure which he was most worried about, mind, the jeep, the gear, or you two.'

'Sophie can never resist a challenge,' Harry added passing them with his arms full of gear. 'You'd have thought Dave would have learned that by now.'

7

Five days later, Lisa was on her knees in the trench, scraping carefully at a charred black layer in the side which had been uncovered as they dug down. The experts among their number had agreed it marked a sizeable fire, which squared with the few blackened stones that could still be found among the grass and bracken on the mound which was the castle site. They had uncovered postholes, marking the sites of buildings, and a few shards of blackened wood, but so far, no trace of stone building remains. 'I wouldn't expect any,' Dave had remarked. 'There wouldn't be stone dwellings outside the castle itself. Pity we can't excavate up there,' he added, casting a covetous glance at the castle mound. 'It's not a Scottish Heritage site, and the landowner has refused permission. Foreign invaders – curse of the Highlands!'

There had been no spectacular finds, to the disappointment of the eight novice diggers, though careful riddling of the excavated soil had produced fragments of bone, shells and shards of pottery especially from the area they had identified as the 'midden' or spoil heap. Lisa herself had unearthed one of the largest of the shards, and lovingly brushed it clean before handing it over to the supervisors. Everyone was secretly hoping for an intact skeleton, or even a skull, but they had been disappointed. Despite the lack of headline finds, Lisa had thoroughly enjoyed her week. The weather continued cold, but quite sunny, and although the nights were freezing, she had slept well inside the top-quality sleeping bag and sturdy lightweight tent that had been two of the best of her eighteenth birthday presents.

In the evenings they gathered in the 'Caff', the largest of the tents, furnished with a long trestle table, benches and basic cooking facilities at the far end, to check the day's finds, or just to relax and chat over food and hot drinks. On a couple of nights, unusually free of wind, they had lit a bonfire outside and gathered round it. One of the remaining Aberdeen students, Craig, produced a ukulele, and they happily joined in singing folk songs and favourite hits. Lisa soon found that her voice was in demand, given the largely male ensemble, and she was persuaded to borrow the instrument, which she could strum a little, and sing a traditional Geordie ballad, '*Ma Bonny Lad*'. She was aware that Matthew, sitting on the far side, could also sing well. 'It's a Welsh thing,' he admitted next day. 'We had a big choir at school, and singing was considered almost as cool as rugby.' In the second night's sing-song, after she had followed her earlier success with the plaintive '*Water o' Tyne*', he was persuaded into a harmonised duet of '*Scarborough Fair*', to whoops and loud applause.

'Pity you're not at Aberdeen,' said Craig, who had accompanied them. 'The three of us could go busking!' Lisa registered Matthew's look of horror with a grin. 'Do you play anything?'

'Piano,' said Lisa. 'Not much use for busking!'

'Guitar – acoustic,' Matthew admitted.

'Me too, but the uke's easier for travels and digs. Guitar's always a hit at uni, isn't it?'

'Er – yeah,' said Matthew, not wanting to admit that he had left his at home. Lisa guessed! Craig was continuing to play gently and automatically as he chatted, which Lisa thought sounded lovely. She wished she could hear him play his guitar. And Matt too! One day, perhaps….

One of the best things about the dig, she reflected in her tent at night, was the easy-going nature of the relationships in the group. She got on well with Sophie but being accepted as 'one of the boys' was also rather nice. She'd suffered, from time to time, from the cliques and falling-out in groups of girls at school and found this casual camaraderie a pleasant change.

That evening, as she climbed stiffly to her feet, realising to her surprise that the sun was going down, she saw Matthew coming towards her. He extended a hand to haul her out of the trench. 'There's something I want to show you,' he said. 'We've got time before supper. It's up on the castle mound.'

'What is it?'

'You'll see!'

'OK, I'll just get the worst of the mud off my hands and fetch my gloves. Won't be a minute.' He watched her run across the site to the washing tent, then got his binoculars out of their case and trained them on the mountain slopes ahead while he waited. There were deer further up among the crags.

When Lisa got back, the two of them set off, past the abandoned trenches, and scrambled over rocks and tussocks to the flattened top of the castle mound. They had all been up to scrape among the worked stones, and lament that they couldn't undertake a proper dig. 'I bet there are dungeons under here!' Phil had remarked on the first night, and the possibility of chained skeletons had haunted all of them. It was so frustrating that they couldn't excavate! But it was the view, not the potential treasures beneath their feet, that was interesting Matthew this evening.

He led Lisa to a spot on the mound where they could see right up the narrow valley at right angles to their own. There were more trees up there, but no sign of a track. A small burn ran through it. He gave Lisa his binoculars. 'I was watching a heron in the burn yesterday evening,' he said, as she adjusted the focus. 'And when it flew up I followed it with the binoculars, and that's when I spotted it. There's a really odd-shaped hill right at the end of the valley – can you see it? The top's smooth and domed! Got it?'

'Oh yes, I see it! Looks a bit like a huge bald head.'

Matthew chuckled. 'That's the one. Can you see anything else?'

'What sort of thing?'

'Smoke.'

'Smoke?' Lisa lowered the binoculars and stared at him. 'You saw *smoke* up there yesterday?'

'Sort of irregular puffs, rising from that hilltop. Not like a column of smoke from a fire. Let me have another look.' He peered through his binoculars, then shook his head. 'Nothing tonight. Probably a hiker or someone. But we've seen no one else while we've been here, and that valley's a bit of a dead end. I checked the map when I got back. Here.' He handed the binoculars back.

Lisa took them and stared longingly at the far-away hill. Finally, she lowered the binoculars and sighed. 'It can't be, of course!' she said. 'It's just that – well – smoke.... dragons... lonely valley in the Highlands....'

'I know,' Matthew said sympathetically. 'Sorry to raise your hopes, but it did seem a bit odd. I thought it was worth checking out.'

'Let's keep looking anyway,' Lisa said, handing back his binoculars. 'These are great, by the way. That's next on my Christmas list. Evening you said you saw it? Let's come and look again tomorrow.'

That was typical of Lisa, Matthew thought as they made their way down to the camp for supper. She never gave up!

They were disappointed next day. In the afternoon it started to rain, and by evening a steady drizzle set in and the mist came down over the tops. There was no chance of a decent fire. Although they all stayed longer than usual in the Caff, chatting and drinking coffee, tea or beer, everyone retired to their tents early to catch up on sleep. There was only one day of the dig left, Lisa thought as she settled down in her sleeping bag. Probably no chance of any further investigation of mysterious smoke up the valley.

Unusually she woke in the middle of the night. Shining the torch on her watch, she sighed – three thirty, and she needed to go to the loo. Too much tea after supper! She had managed to avoid a night-time trip to the loo-tent so far, but not tonight. Cursing the fact that rain was still drumming on the roof of her tent, she groped for her anorak and boots, unzipped the flap and crawled out. The thin beam of her torch was of some use in finding the way, but the mist didn't help, and the rain was still quite heavy. She reached her destination safely and was making her way back to bed, following her own footprints, when a strange noise above made her stop, heart pounding. It was like nothing she had ever heard before, slow and rhythmic, coming from the shrouded air above her. She swung her torch beam up and around but could see nothing but mist. The sound stopped but the mist above her head seemed to swirl eerily; then she heard it again, but softer, further away, a heavy beat. As it died away, she realised that she was holding her breath and shaking. She needed to get to the safety of her tent – now! She was about to run, but common sense kicked in. She mustn't slip, and she mustn't lose her own trail of footprints. She couldn't risk trying to climb into the wrong tent, even though it would be comforting to find another person!

It seemed to take far longer than the way out, but it was not actually many minutes before she reached the open flap of her tent and crawled in, zipping it firmly before she peeled off her boots and anorak. Although she felt as though she'd been up for ages, her sleeping bag was still warm. Her violent shivering eased, and she fell into an uneasy sleep, waking several times with a start to imagined noises outside. But the camp was silent as the rain gradually eased to a drizzle.

By morning it had stopped, and a weak sun was forcing its way through the remnants of the mist. The site was muddy, and some pools had formed in the trenches. The students gathered in the main tent for breakfast and got their orders for this final day. Tomorrow they would pack up and head back to civilisation; meanwhile work was needed on the charts and notes and the labelling of the finds, which would be packed carefully and transported to the labs in Aberdeen and Edinburgh for full analysis. There would be time for some final digging in the last trench. To Lisa's delight, she and Matthew were both allocated a morning in the trench, and she was careful to pick a spot near to his, where they could converse without being overheard. As she scraped with her trowel, she related the story of her night-time fright.

'I've never heard a sound like it before,' she finished. 'It was pretty scary, with the mist and the rain, and nothing to see at all. I was beginning to wonder if I'd imagined it when I woke this morning. I thought if I told you about it, it might seem more real.'

'Could it have been a large bird? Swans and geese make quite a weird noise when they fly, but they would be unlikely, up here in the dark. We've seen eagles around, but it would be odd to have an eagle flying low at night.

They usually roost, and they tend to keep away from people anyway.'

'A large owl perhaps? I didn't hear any hooting, though.'

'No. Owls are quite silent when they fly. You wouldn't hear heavy flapping. You're sure it wasn't the wind?'

'There wasn't any wind for once – just mist and drizzle.'

'No idea what it could have been, then. Except an over-active imagination and wishful thinking.'

'Wishful thinking…Huh!'

He glanced sideways at her, noting her scowl while still diligently scraping with his trowel. 'You never give up!'

'Never! And I've had another idea. Tell you later. Can I come birdwatching again this evening?'

'Of course! Though *another idea* sounds ominous! Should I be worried?' He grinned, and Lisa reflected that he had come out of his shell a good deal on this trip. Less of a professor and more of a … an explorer? Perhaps it was the effect of a week's growth of stubble. All the boys had abandoned shaving, with varied results; being so dark had given Matthew a distinct advantage. It rather suited him. She hoped he'd like her idea.

A yell of triumph sounded from the other end of the trench. A find! They stopped talking and concentrated on digging, neither of them wanting to be outdone on this last day. But as she scraped and sieved, Lisa thought that it was a good thing that Matthew had established himself as a keen birder as well as an archaeologist. No-one would think anything of it if they headed off with binoculars before supper.

In the afternoon, Matthew, who was known to be painstakingly neat and accurate, was tasked with sorting, bagging and labelling specimens in the Caff, while Sophie carefully marked the location of each one on their sketch maps and charts. Harry was using the expensive departmental camera to complete the photographic record. The two academics from Aberdeen, with a trio of postgrads arrived to supervise the final work on the site, which would be restored to as near its original state as possible. Dave Andrews joined them to discuss the findings and possible conclusions. Meanwhile Lisa and the remaining Edinburgh students took up spades and began filling in their trenches as soon as the records were finished. 'Sorry about this,' said Harry cheerfully. 'We'd usually have a mechanical digger for this job, not slave labour. That's the snag of working in the wilds. Archaeology isn't nearly as glamorous as it looks on telly.' He proceeded to the next trench with his camera, ignoring the rude hand-gestures that marked his departure.

After the afternoon of doing the donkey-work expected of novices, Lisa was tired and muddy; but she had done her fair share, and felt rewarded, in a perverse way, that none of the boys had offered to take over her spade. A dig seemed to be a place of gender equality, which was nice, she thought, even though her back was aching and she longed for the luxury of a hot shower. As they were finishing the final trench, Matthew strolled over, looking far too clean, and accepted with good humour the insults heaped on a guy who sat around *labelling* while REAL blokes did the hard graft.

Paul spotted the binoculars he was carrying. 'And now, I suppose, you're off *birdwatching*!'

'That's right!' said Matthew, cheerfully. 'Now that I've checked on the job you've been working on. Yes, looks good. Well done, chaps!' he added, putting on an upper-class-officer voice.

'And me!' said Lisa. 'I did my share! Can I come and see if those eagles are still around?'

'Not with hands that colour,' Matthew retorted, reverting to his normal voice with its Welsh lilt. 'I'll be up there when you're clean.' He headed off towards the castle site, and Lisa, grinning, set off to find hot water. Paul, commenting that '*Some* chaps have decent manners!' offered to put her spade away.

Ten minutes later she scrambled up the slope to find Matthew sitting on a rock, binoculars trained on the lochan, where two coots were nest-building in the reeds. 'I haven't looked at Old Baldy,' he said, without looking up. 'I left it to you. I know you think there might be a dragon up there, and you need to be the first to see it. I mean him. Or her!' He lowered the glasses and grinned at her. 'Sorry about the mucky-hands comment! You looked so muddy I couldn't resist.'

Lisa waved clean hands at him. 'That's OK. You're now considered the sort of ill-mannered guy that no decent feminist would *ever* bother with. Excellent cover! Can I really have first look up the valley?'

'Hmmm. Better watch myself!' he said, half joking, handing the binoculars over.

She trained them on the distant hilltop, lit now with the apricot rays of the setting sun. She swept them around the area, concentrating, then sighed. 'Nothing! Oh, wait a minute – I think there's some smoke. No – yes! A thin wavering stream – you can hardly see it against the hill. You look! Tell me I'm seeing things.'

Matthew took the binoculars and focussed. 'I think you're right,' he said thoughtfully. 'But that's nothing like the puffs I saw the other night. It looks more like a camp fire, but it's very faint. In fact, the sun's gone in, and I can't see it at all now.'

'That settles it,' said Lisa, very firmly, as if daring him to disagree. 'I want to go up that valley and see if there's anything there. Smoke – two lots – and those flapping wings must mean *something*. And anyway, it's a lovely valley! I looked at the map last night, and there's quite a big loch up there, so there should be lots of interesting birds even if there are no …' She looked round theatrically and whispered, '*dragons…* What do you think?'

'How? We can't stay on here. We'll have to leave with the rest tomorrow. And it's pretty inaccessible without transport.'

'Finn has a car. Well, it really belongs to his step-brother, but he gets to borrow it. It's pretty old, but it would get us as far as the hostel'

'Oh, I see! You're planning to tell him about your new set of *feelings* and get him to come with you?'

'Come with *us*. You want to come dragon-hunting, don't you? I have feelings, you have binoculars and Finn has a car! We all have boots and tents and can cope with camping. Even if I'm totally wrong about the dragons, there'll be plenty of birds. As soon as I can get a signal, I'm ringing Finn and we can start planning a proper expedition. There's the bell for supper. Come on! Don't want to be late.'

She turned and skipped happily down the mound. 'Don't twist an ankle!' Matthew called after her as he followed at a more sensible pace. She turned, made a face at him and carried on. 'And by the way!' he added. 'It wasn't just your hands! There's quite a lot of the trench on your face too!'

The final supper at the dig was a determinedly cheerful affair. The last trip by jeep to the hostel to replenish supplies had returned with several bottles of mulled wine, which was filling the tent with a spicy aroma as it heated up. The remnants of their fruit were being chopped and added to the pan by Sophie as Lisa entered, having washed her face and put on the cleanest of her sweaters. She peered into the pan and sniffed appreciatively. 'Perfect! A last-night celebration!'

'Back to civilisation and non-stop social media tomorrow.'

Lisa wrinkled her nose. 'Can't say I've missed it!'

'Most of them have though!' Sophie grinned. 'We've seen them sneaking up the hillside, hoping for a signal! But you've really enjoyed it, haven't you? Dave's most impressed. He wants you to switch to archaeology as your main subject. He reckons you're a natural. And he doesn't dish out random compliments, believe me!'

'*Really*?'

'True! Think about it. You've the rest of the year to make your mind up.'

'Wow, I will! This is a gorgeous spot. I'd like to explore a bit more sometime,' she added casually. 'Is the hostel where we parked the bus ever open for hikers?'

'No, the YHA abandoned it when the new landowner started being difficult. The old lairds were usually OK, as long as you didn't disturb the grouse, but some of these new ones are a complete pain.'

'I suppose anyone could park a car there and walk up the valley, like we did?'

'Bit of a risk. If the Factor found it, he'd probably set it alight. He's a cantankerous old sod. He'll likely be along tomorrow morning to see us off the premises. This looks hot enough. Fill up your mug before the mob. Bar's open!' she shouted, and there was a surge of students towards them. Lisa, her mug full, eased herself out of the way. That had been a useful bit of conversation! There would be plenty to discuss with Finn as soon as she could get hold of him.

The following morning, the camp was struck, the tents packed, the Land Rover loaded, and the Edinburgh contingent set off, bidding farewell to the remaining Aberdeen group who would finish restoring the site and take down the last tents before leaving themselves. 'Cheers! Keep up the music!' Craig called to Lisa and Matthew as they got ready to leave. The jeep jolted up the track, threatened to founder, but finally got under way in a flurry of muddy water. The walkers shouldered their packs and prepared to follow. They were already thinking longingly of hot showers and reliable signals. Sophie, walking ahead of Lisa, turned and pointed up the hill. A short craggy man, leaning on a hefty stick, was standing very still watching them leave. He almost looked as though he was a part of the hill.

'Told you!' she said. 'Foreigners not welcome in this glen!'

'Perhaps we'd better not wave!' Lisa remarked. Already she was plotting her return, but she decided not to mention the fact. She needed to talk to Finn!

8

It was late afternoon when they finally arrived back in Edinburgh. Most of them had dozed off in the minibus as soon as it turned off the narrow road and they were back onto smoother tarmac. They dropped Sophie and Harry in Stirling; as there were still three weeks to go before lectures started again, they were all heading their separate ways from Edinburgh, either that evening, or the following day. Lisa was fortunate in that her room in Hall was not required over the break – sometimes the University let out rooms for conferences – and she hauled her pack wearily up the stairs and headed for the shower. She had arranged for her mother to collect her the following day, as public transport between Edinburgh and her rural Northumberland home was either erratic or non-existent.

She had already filled a case with washing, even before adding the muddy contents of her rucksack.

The shower was blissful, and when her hair was finally unplaited, conditioned, rinsed clean and blow-dried she felt like a different person, energised and ready to join the remainder of the group for a meal at the Pear Tree, as arranged on the way home. They were all reluctant to break up the camaraderie of the dig. Dressed in the very last of her clean clothes and wearing make-up for the first time for a week, she met Matthew on the corner. He gave a theatrical double-take at the sight of her respectable appearance, and she stared at him critically before commenting, 'You've shaved it off!'

He shuddered. 'I couldn't wait!'

'It was coming on nicely. I rather liked it! I bet some of the others have kept theirs. Probably the ones with the least chance of a decent result. Phil hasn't a hope!'

'Did you get hold of Finn?' he asked, changing the subject, as they strolled down the road together. Edinburgh seemed quite balmy after the Highlands!

'No,' Lisa admitted. 'I thought of trying, but I'll be seeing him tomorrow. Better to talk to him. I can be much more persuasive in person.'

'I believe you!' He hesitated, then added, 'But I have a feeling he'd rather *not* have me tagging along. I don't mind if you'd rather go by yourselves.'

Lisa shot him a sideways glance. 'No, I want you to come. Three of us, that's the deal! He'll be fine. I told you, we're not going out together. He's more like a brother really. I've known him for years; we went to school together, parents are old friends – that kind of thing. I'll message you as soon as I've sorted it out and we can fix dates.'

'If you're sure.... It would be great to explore that valley. Glen I mean – Sophie corrected me. It's a *cwm* in Wales.'

As they reached the pub, Lisa stopped. 'Come over to my room when we get back. I've something to show you. Just ...' She paused, but Matthew was ahead of her.

'... be discreet. Rumour mill! I'll be careful.' He grinned and held open the door with a flourish. 'Let's see how well the rest of them scrub up!'

An ironic chorus of whistles greeted Lisa's appearance, with comments such as, 'She *is* a girl – thought it was wishful thinking!' 'Wow, lipstick!' and 'I'd no idea your hair was that colour!' and she and Matthew joined the group, looking forward to a relaxed evening of jokes, reminiscences and decent food.

On the way home, they were joined by Paul, also making his way back to Hall for the night, so Lisa had no opportunity to remind Matthew of his promise to visit. She had almost decided that he had forgotten, and was thinking longingly of her bed, when there was a soft knock at the door.

'Come in!'

'Sorry, couldn't get Paul to stop talking! He's decided to keep working on the beard, you'll be pleased to hear. What did you want to show me?'

'These!' Lisa spread six water-colour paintings on her desk. 'These are the original pictures that Megan painted. I showed you the photos on my phone, remember? She did them from memory, obviously, but they're really good, and pretty well exactly as I remember the dragons too.'

'Wow! These *are* good!' Matthew picked one up and gazed at a menacing dragon, reared on his hind legs and breathing fire. 'Yes, I really think that's the one we saw! He wasn't as big and bright as that, though I suppose the light was going when I saw him.'

'That's Des, and he seemed pretty big and bright in the cellar! This one was my favourite. Emily.' She pointed to a second picture – a friendlier-looking dragon, with outstretched wings, shaded in blue, purple and pink, and gazed at it critically. 'I'm not sure she's got her colour quite right – she was bluer than that – but it's Megan's memory, not mine. This was *her* favourite.' She pointed to the smallest painting, where a little golden dragon crouched on the branch of a tree.

'They are fantastic!' Matthew said, studying each of the pictures in turn.

'So, now that you know exactly what we're looking for, and how *incredibly* fantastic they are,' said Lisa, collecting the pictures up and sliding them carefully into a large envelope, 'you HAVE to come and help us find them again.'

'OK, I give in! I'll admit it – I'd love to come. I won't see you tomorrow morning – I'm off on an early train. Takes all day to get home. But message me when you've talked to Finn. Assuming he agrees to include me in the expedition.'

'Don't worry - he will!' said Lisa.

EMILY

1

'THEY'VE GONE!' Desmond called triumphantly as he landed outside the cave. He was little changed from the threatening fire-breather of Lisa's memory and Megan's picture, though the flamboyant painted stripes on his wings had faded with the years, and he was perhaps a little plumper. But his love of exploring was as strong as ever, though these days he always took his beloved Emily travelling with him. She was now fully grown, the purple-blue of her scales a little darker, and she and Des had established a home together in the cave further up the mountain that she had discovered with her mother many years before.

It was late afternoon and Duncan was inside, debating with Gwen whether it was safe to light the fire, but Emily rushed out to hear his news. Des hugged her in triumph. 'Every single one of them!' he declared, as the other dragons emerged. 'Most headed away this morning, but then the rest packed up the last of their junk and left later. The old guy came down and poked around, but then he went too. We're rid of them!' Four deep sighs of relief sent huffs of dragon-smoke into the air. In Emily's case, there was also a tinge of regret.

Ever since Des and Emily, flying high in the early morning on the way home from one of their expeditions, had spotted the tents of the archaeologists at the old castle site three weeks before, Duncan and Gwen – especially Duncan - had been very worried. In all the years they had lived in this glen, no human had been seen; only the 'old guy', always dressed in brown and almost like a moving part of the hillside, had occasionally been spotted down in the main valley, but he had never ventured up the glen, not even as far as the loch, and there had certainly never been any danger of his catching a glimpse of a dragon and spreading the news that dragons were real and hiding out in the Highlands.

In the face of this new emergency, Des had organised reconnaissance. Knowing the land around like his own talons, he had established a base in the shelter of a rocky outcrop high on the hill overlooking the castle mound. From there, well hidden, he could keep a watch on the Humans below, ready to warn the rest of the family if any ventured up the glen towards their hidden cave. But nobody had. He had got rather bored, and the three weeks seemed very long, even though Duncan had relieved him from time to time, and Emily had crept carefully down each day to bring food and keep watch with him. She had always been fascinated by Humans, especially since her secret meeting with four children some years before. She had wanted to sneak closer to the camp-site to spy on them, but for once Des had been the cautious one.

'At first, I thought there wasn't much danger,' he said. 'They only seem interested in what's in the ground, for some reason. They're digging. Can't think why. They don't eat worms and roots, do they?' He considered Emily an expert on Humans, because of the books she had read, even though, as a Traveller, and a frequent risk-taker, he had seen them at closer quarters than most dragons.

'I don't think so. They do dig for food sometimes, though. Like tatties. They grow under the ground.'

'The place looks typically Human now,' Des remarked. 'They have a thing about squares! But it's not just digging any more. A few days ago, one of them started looking all around with those binoccy things you told me about. He seems to like watching deer, but they're keeping well away from this rock because we're here, so that's safe enough. He even stood on the castle ruins, peering up our Glen. Good thing Ben's not awake – that WOULD give them something to think about. A mountain with eyes!'

'I still don't think *these* Humans are any danger to us,' Emily said thoughtfully. 'There are no wire fences and none of those dragon-machines like we saw at the old glen. They were horribly noisy and made a dreadful mess of the land. These people have tents, and it says in my books they're only used for what they call 'holidays', so they're not going to stay for ever. They're not building anything. Couldn't we creep down after dark? We might find out what they're up to. Go on! You're dying of curiosity too – you wouldn't want Tom and Ollie to say you're getting old....'

'They say it all the time anyway. Especially since I settled down with you.' He pulled her into a hug with one wing and heaved a heavy sigh. 'Camping out on my own like this is like my old Traveller days. I wish they'd go! It's much cosier in the cave with you.'

Emily snuggled closer. 'I'll stay a bit longer tonight.' She peered cautiously at the dig site. 'They've all disappeared into that big tent, so it's safe at the moment. Stretch your wings!'

Des peered into the gloaming too. 'No, they're coming out again. What *are* they doing? Oh, I know! They're lighting a fire! Trying to, anyway. They're not much good at it, are they?'

'Shall we fly down and offer to help?' Emily giggled. 'Oh, I think it's worked!' Down in the valley the bonfire had caught reluctantly, and as the flames sprang up and the smell of the wood-smoke drifted towards the watching dragons, they saw the Humans, looking very small and not at all dangerous, gather in a ring around it. The sound of laughter came to their ears, and then singing. Emily gasped, and her eyes filled with tears.

'Des, they're just like us!' she whispered, sniffing. 'Do you remember when you took us to the seaside, years ago, with the Gramps? We sat round a fire like that in the gloaming, while Grandad told stories and Gran sang.'

'Of course I do! And I seem to remember that we nearly got discovered by Humans that time too! My fault – I should have scouted more thoroughly. I was young and foolish then!'

'I sneaked away and waved to the girl on the train. Phoebe. The one who wrote the message in the sand. She saw me, but I'm sure she never gave me away. Just like the others we met in Angie's Castle. Des, these Humans are the same kind – I'm sure of it. I wish we could find out.'

Des looked tempted, then shook his head sadly. 'There are far too many of them down there. It would be different if there were just one or two. Daren't risk it. And think of your Dad. He'd have a fit!' On this point Emily had to agree. By the second week of the Human invasion, Duncan had been threatening to vacate their beloved cave and fly off in search of a safer home. Fortunately, his wife had persuaded him to wait, and after lengthy argument, Duncan had agreed. He had, however, moved their stores from the main cave and hidden them carefully behind the firewood in the Bone Cave at the back just in case they had to clear the place and leave in a hurry; an arrangement which caused great irritation to everyone else when it came to cooking in the evening.

Des's main concern for the last weeks had been that their stores of food, depleted at the end of the winter, were even lower than usual, and foraging without the risk of being seen by the campers was difficult. He had tried some night hunting, but it was much harder than by day. Fortunately, he had spotted a covey of grouse preparing to roost high on the opposite mountain in sight of his hiding place late one evening and had raided it under cover of darkness. It had been hard work flying home with a heavy load of dead birds, but he had managed, and the resulting stew had been worth it. Everyone was sick of bulrush roots, which was a staple food by the end of winter, especially Emily, who had never liked them. Now, with the Humans gone, it looked as though the problem of their supplies might be eased a little.

That evening, as the sun set behind the mountains, the dragons gathered for supper in a much more cheerful frame of mind. Even Duncan seemed more relaxed. 'Right, now they've gone it should be safe for Alice and the others to come,' Emily said firmly, when supper was nearly over. 'It's far too quiet here, with even Tom away. Isn't it Lily?' she asked her young sister, who had been more than usually bored and bolshie while the Human threat hung over them. Lily rolled expressive eyes in agreement and nodded but carried on eating.

'Perhaps we should wait a bit in case they come back,' Duncan said cautiously, causing Lily to roll her eyes even more and mutter 'Oh *Da..ad*!' through a last mouthful.

'At least we'll be safe to send a Huff,' Gwen said serenely, bringing nettle tea. 'Then they can decide when to come. I've checked their camp site, and it's clear of snow and drying up nicely. There's been no trace of Humans there.'

'Good weather for the Gloaming Huff tonight,' said Des, getting to his feet. 'I'll go up to Ben and send the news. Coming Emily?' Emily gulped the last of her tea and the two of them flew to settle on the smooth top of Ben's head. Ben McIlwhinnie, the ancient Mountain Giant who guarded their cave and protected the Glen, had been asleep as usual through the winter months. Indeed, he was difficult to wake even in the height of summer, and with his huge eyes closed and his breathing so faint that even dragons could scarcely hear it, he looked just like part of the landscape. Several bushes and rowan trees had taken root on and around him. Some years before he had actually risen and walked south to save the dragon family from terrible danger, but since then, apart from occasional wakeful days in high summer, he had snoozed and slept through the years. Emily, who loved Ben, huffed a hopeful kiss at him as she flew past his nose, but there was no response.

It was obvious that Alice and her family, away to the South, had been watching out for a signal, because as soon as Des's cheerful ***'all safe humans gone'*** was huffed into the deepening blue of the sky, Emily spotted the far-away smoke and read the return message ***'good coming in 2 or 3 days tom and ollie gone again'***. ***'can you contact them'*** Des huffed back and received the answer ***'yes'***. A couple of farewell kisses told Emily that it was Alice huffing the messages. She beamed at Des as they finished the Huff. 'It'll be lovely to see Alice again. I miss her a lot, even though I've got you!'

Des grinned, put a wing round her and they sat close together, gazing down the Glen as the dusk deepened and the first stars appeared. They could hear the stream, bubbling with melted snow, hurtling down towards the loch further down the valley, and the shrill voice of Lily, raised in argument with her parents, travelled up from the cave below. Emily sighed. 'I hope she cheers up when she hears the others are coming back.'

'She'll be pleased to see Georgie, at least.' Des slid a sideways glance at Emily. 'Why don't we head home for a bit of peace and quiet?'

While the Human threat remained, the two of them had moved back into the big cave under Ben's enormous chair, where Emily and her family had settled years ago. It was safer to be together, with the thought that they could use the smaller hidden cave up the mountain as a refuge for all of them if there was any danger of discovery. Now the threat was removed, Des reasoned, there was no need to stay, and he was looking forward to having Emily to himself, away from Duncan's fretting and Lily's outbursts of temper. The bolshie wee dragon was now a teenager!

Emily turned her head and smiled at him. 'Yes, let's,' she said fondly. 'I'll just go down and let Mum know. Back in a minute.' She huffed him a kiss and disappeared. Des stretched his wings, staring around the mountains and the Glen. There was a faint bellow from a stag on the slopes above him, and a large owl flew silently past on its way down to the woods below. The bats, who had always roosted in the cave, were already swooping and hunting, and they greeted Emily with high squeaking cries as she flew back to join him.

'Dad was doubtful, but Mum understood,' she said as they prepared to fly. 'She admitted she'll be glad to see the others back too!'

'Right, let's be off!' said Des. 'Race you home!' They took off together and soared up the mountain, wheeling and looping in the joy of flight and freedom.

2

Des slept soundly that night, enjoying a decent bed after three weeks sleeping out on the hill, but Emily tossed and turned beside him, scattering heather. She emerged rather late, and found Des making breakfast on the wide rock ledge a little way below the mouth of their cave. It was halfway up a rocky gorge whose sides were so sheer that only winged dragons or birds could access it, so it was a good deal safer than Ben's cave, which Humans *would* be able to reach and explore, if they ever discovered it.

'It felt as though you were fighting with your heather last night,' Des remarked, passing her some porridge, to which he had added his favourite chilli. 'Or me, perhaps. Missing your old bedroom?'

'No, I was thinking about the Gramps. They've been in my mind ever since we heard those Humans singing round the fire. Especially Nan. I haven't been very successful with the Quest she gave me, have I? I don't deserve the pendant I inherited.' She looped the silver pendant on one talon and gazed at it sadly. It had been Nan's parting gift and she never took it off. 'She wanted us to try to find a way of contacting Humans and making a link, instead of hiding away and being afraid all the time.'

'Well, Old George and your Grandad went to Ireland to try and make contact, and you said you thought they had managed it. But we never heard any more.'

'It's such a long time since I had a Call from George,' Emily said sadly. 'Mum hasn't heard either. I think he must be dead.' She was referring to the mysterious psychic gift that allowed her to communicate with certain other dragons over many miles. She had inherited it from her mother and grandmother, and Old George, Alice's grandfather had the gift as well; but it was rare, and nobody else in either dragon family seemed to have it. 'Have you been putting chilli in the porridge again?' she added crossly. 'You know I'd rather have honey.'

'It was only a bit!' Des said defensively but decided not to argue. He passed her a mug of nettle tea in the hope it would cheer her up, but she was still frowning.

'I STILL think we should have tried to contact those people digging by the old castle. I'm sure they were the right sort of Human. It's the best chance we've *ever* had, and now they've gone. I don't suppose they'll come back. They took their tents away and even filled in those square holes they made. I've failed Nan. Again!' She sounded unusually upset and angry, and Des sympathised, though he still believed they had been right to stay hidden.

'D'you want to take a flight down to the castle? We could see if they've left any clues behind. I'd like to find out what those squares mean as well. We needn't tell your Dad!'

Emily looked more cheerful. 'Yes, let's! Finish your tea and we'll go.'

'Er … I didn't mean this *minute*,' Des admitted. 'Better towards evening, just in case that old guy is still hanging around.'

'I think I liked you better when you were young and daring!' Emily retorted. 'OK, this evening. And if you make another excuse, I'll go on my own! I'm going to sort my heather.' She rose and was about to head back into the cave when a harsh croak made both dragons look round. A large raven was flying towards them 'Och, crivens, ye'r back!' it said, through a beakful of twigs. 'Nest's near sorted. Then th'll be eggs, an' wull be countin' 'em carefully, mind!' It flapped up to a ledge a little way along the cliff without waiting for a reply, joined its mate, and added the twigs to the untidy heap that served as their nest.

'As if we'd want to eat *their* eggs! They're such horrible neighbours! I much preferred my bats,' Emily grumbled, and stomped into the cave, leaving Des to do the washing up in the stream below. He was grinning happily to himself. He loved Emily in this belligerent mood!

By the late afternoon, Emily was feeling a good deal more cheerful. She and Des headed down the Glen as the sun set, skirting carefully round the bulk of Ben McIlwhinnie so that the family would not spot them. They knew that Duncan would not approve of their expedition. They flew low over the loch and followed the stream down to the castle site, keeping wary eyes and ears alert for possible danger. But there was no sign of any Human presence. 'The deer are back in the valley,' Des pointed out. 'That's a good sign. Or a bad sign if you *want* to meet a Human, of course,' he added and dodged the fiery huff that Emily sent in his direction.

The two dragons landed on the stones of the castle site and looked around carefully. 'They don't seem to have disturbed this,' Emily said thoughtfully. 'Let's go to the place where they put their tents. I'm sure there's no one left, so it's quite *safe*.' Without waiting for Des to agree, she took off and he followed close behind her, scanning the hills around for possible dangers as he went. The evening was darkening, but the square patches of ground were clearly visible, even though it was obvious that the Humans had tried hard to cover their tracks. Deep ridged boot-marks in the damp ground and lighter patches of grass where the tents had been were all clear to see as they flew low over the site. The dragons landed by the blackened circle that had been the diggers' bonfire. 'They left some wood behind,' Des remarked. 'We might as well take that back with us. Doesn't look as though there's anything else, though.'

'Which is odd,' Emily pointed out. 'You know how much rubbish Humans tend to leave lying around. These people have cleared up very carefully. I'm sure they were the right sort of Human. Perhaps they'll come back,' she added hopefully, standing in the middle of the flattened grass where the largest tent had been. She shut her eyes and imagined the Humans as she had seen them that evening, sitting round the fire and singing, just like dragons.

'Here's something!' Des's voice broke into her thoughts. He had been rooting in the bracken at the edge of the site, and held up a white plastic water bottle, with a black carrying strap. He shook it and heard the sloshing of liquid. He gripped the top with a talon and tried to prise it off, without success. Emily took it from him and unscrewed the lid, with difficulty.

'It goes round and round,' she explained, lifting it off and sniffing the contents. 'I've read about it. I think this is just water.'

Des took it from her. 'Better taste and see,' he said cautiously, tilting the bottle. 'Yes, it's water!' He sounded slightly disappointed, Emily thought. 'But the thing might be useful. We could fill it up and tie it to a talon for long journeys. Especially when we fly a long way over the sea. We always get thirsty, and seawater tastes horrible.'

'Let's keep looking while there's enough light to see.' Emily began to work her way around the edge of the tent site, but the clear-up had been thorough. As the spring advanced and the grass and bracken grew, all traces of these Humans would disappear, she thought. Already their presence was beginning to seem rather like a dream. She hoped there would be enough evidence left for Tom, Ollie and Alice to believe their story when they returned to the Glen.

Des had been investigating the mysterious squares. Some attempt had been made to put back the covering of turf, but there were enough bare patches for him to scrape soil away with a talon to try and work out what the digging had been about. After a few minutes he gave up and tried another patch, but nothing in the damp earth gave him any clue, until the tip of a talon hit something sharp. It wasn't a stone, but a small flat oblong, shiny when he wiped the mud off on the grass and covered in squiggles. He called softly to Emily. 'Is this writing?' he asked, passing the object over. Emily took it and peered in the dimming light, frowning as she tried to make out the letters. She turned it over and exclaimed in delight. 'There's a Human in it!' she said.

'What! Where?' Des sounded horrified and came over to take it from her. 'How did it get there? It's only a little one. Good thing too!'

Emily giggled. 'It's only a picture! I've seen them in books. They're not dangerous. This is a man, I think, and this writing might be his name. P-H-I-L… I don't know this word, or these long ones on the other side. This is a great find!' She beamed at him, though Des wasn't clear why she was so excited. It didn't explain what the Humans were doing in the Glen; and even more important, whether they would be coming back!

Emily was still peering at the card clutched in her talon. 'Mum might be able to read these words,' she said thoughtfully, but Des interrupted. 'Better not! Your Dad will go on and on about taking risks.'

'P'raps you're right,' Emily agreed reluctantly. 'But I might see if Alice can work it out.'

'That would be OK, I suppose. We'd better get back. It's getting too dark to see anything else tonight.'

'Pity Tom and Ollie aren't here,' Emily said, as they took off, Des carrying a bundle of firewood, and Emily with the water bottle and the precious card clutched tightly in a talon. 'They'll be mad that they've missed the chance to spy on all those Humans digging here. I bet Ollie would have sneaked down and spied on them properly.'

'And then Tom would have followed, and both would have ended up in a zoo!' Des warned. 'It's a wonder they haven't been caught before now, the risks they take. Don't you dare mention the word *old*!' he added as they skirted Ben McIlwhinnie on their way home.

Emily sniggered. 'Can't help thinking it!' she taunted and dodged the sweep of his tail as he pursued her up the hillside, huffing dire threats and curses.

LISA

Lisa lost no time in laying her summer scheme before Finn. As soon as she arrived home, she helped to unload the car, put on the first batch of washing, enjoyed ecstatic greetings from their two elderly Labradors and revelled in a late and leisurely lunch, with homemade soup, fresh crusty bread and real coffee. She and her mum had exchanged the term's news during the car journey, her dad would not be home until the evening, and Charlie would be late home after football training at school. There was nothing to prevent her going round to Finn's house and dragging him out for a walk.

Finn listened to the long and detailed account of the week's dig. He was interested in their finds and chuckled over Lisa's descriptions of the mud, the weather, Sophie's wild driving, the lengths her techie-minded colleagues would go to find the smallest signal and the best and worst of camp cooking. She decided not to mention the duet with Matthew and waited until the old relaxed comradeship had re-established itself before broaching the subject of a summer expedition. Near the end of their circuit, they reached the pond on the edge of the woodland, the scene of their encounter with five dragons one wet Sunday years before and sat on a fallen log in the last rays of the sun. Enjoying their joint memory, it was easier to bring up the possibilities of the Highland glen and her plans for dragon-hunting in the summer. She instinctively played down Matthew's role in a possible expedition until Finn was committed to the idea.

Finn shook his head over her wildly optimistic belief that finding the dragons was a near-certainty. 'You haven't got much to go on!' he remarked. 'Smoke in the distance could be anything.'

'What about the flapping wings in the night?'

'Dark and spooky night? Wishful thinking?'

'That's more or less what Matt said,' Lisa admitted, saw Finn's frown and decided she had been tactless. She rushed on persuasively. 'But whether there are dragons there or not, it's the most gorgeous place, Finn. Wild and lonely and full of fantastic wildlife. We saw deer and eagles and mountain hares. We didn't have time to explore beyond the dig site, but further up the glen looked even better. The map showed a fairly big loch, and what looked like a gorge further up. Sophie said it's right off the usual trekking routes in the Highlands. Perfect for proper exploration. Couldn't we go at the beginning of the summer holiday? It will be midsummer, hardly dark at all, and much warmer than when we were there. Great for camping out. Please! I know you'll love it!'

'OK, I admit it does sound a great bit of country, dragons or not. But we can't go then, sorry. Steve's got a trip to Europe planned with three of his work-mates so I can't have the car. Actually, I was planning on staying up in Glasgow for most of the holiday and getting a job. In fact, I wondered if you'd like to come up too - to find work for part of the summer. There'll be room in the flat. I know you can't stay on in Hall in Edinburgh, and it's hopeless trying to find a job round here. What d'you think?'

'Haven't got round to thinking about the summer yet.' She was frowning and distracted, her mind obviously elsewhere. He sighed, realising she was not going to be deflected from planning the possible camping expedition.

'Sorry about your idea, Lisa. Not possible. Have to re-think.'

'Oh, Finn, that's such a pain!' she said. 'If only we were rich enough to hire a car…' They both laughed, realising the impossibility of this solution. 'Matt isn't one of the Edinburgh kids with rich parents either,' she admitted. 'He hasn't got a car, though I think he said he'd passed his driving test.'

Finn knew from long experience that Lisa rarely gave up when she had set her mind on something. This was obviously one of those times. Glancing sideways at her determined frown, he realised that she was already trying to work out possible alternatives. The last thing he wanted was for her to find another way of getting to her glen, which might include Matthew but not himself. Another idea came to him. 'When does your term start again?' he asked suddenly.

'Last week of April. I only have three weeks at home because of the field trip.'

'Same as Glasgow then. Why don't we go for a few days at the very end of this holiday? Have your folks got anything planned for then?'

'No, there's a family get-together over Easter weekend, but that's all, I think. You're brilliant, Finn! 'Course, I've no idea what Matt has planned. He was OK for the summer, but we never thought of *this* holiday. I'll message him straight away and find out.' She almost leapt to her feet in her eagerness.

'Better wait 'til I've checked that I can have the car,' Finn warned. As far as he was concerned, Matthew was still an optional extra.

'OK, let me know tonight as soon as you've asked Steve,' Lisa beamed happily. 'It would be great not to have to wait until summer. Thanks, Finn!' She linked an arm through his as they set off towards home. 'I think I can hear the school bus. Charlie's got football training, but Megan should be on it. I'll say hello to her before I go home. We could take her dragon-hunting too. Why not? She'd love it!'

'It'd be a bit of a squash, with four of us and camping gear. And she'll probably be back at school. They don't have such a long holiday.'

'Suppose that's true. Anyway, the important thing is to see if Matt can make it. I'll sound him out as soon as I get home.'

Finn sighed, but so quietly that Lisa didn't hear. She had caught sight of Megan at the far end of the path and was sprinting ahead to give her a hug and catch up on a term's worth of gossip.

EMILY

1

Leaving Desmond happily helping Gwen and Duncan to spice up a welcome feast, Emily and Lily flew along the hill and across the woodland to the clearing beside the small loch that had been the camp site for the English dragons since they had first come to Scotland. It had become a regular arrangement that they should arrive in the spring, when the danger of snow had passed, and stay until the autumn weather made outdoor living uncomfortable so far north. The passage of the years had brought changes. Old George was no longer with them; he had not been seen since he had travelled to Ireland on a personal quest in the company of Edward, Emily's grandfather. Neither dragon had been willing to grow old quietly, becoming a burden to their families, but they were sorely missed. Every time she visited the campsite when their friends returned after a winter away, Emily pictured the wise and kindly Old George sitting by the fire and felt a pang of loss.

Fortunately, there was no chance of dwelling on sad memories when she was with Lily, whose thoughts were all of the coming summer and the anticipated arrival of her best friend, Georgie. She insisted that the two of them should first inspect the old tree-house, now rather dilapidated, but still used as a private den by the two youngest dragons.

'We'd better mend that bit of roof,' she said, gazing up at the patch of sky visible through a hole. 'And we need a new door. The old bracken's blown away. I can do that now, and Georgie can do the roof when he arrives.'

'The bracken will be too dry and brittle,' Emily said. 'You need to wait for new fronds to grow.' As one of the original builders, she considered herself the expert, but as usual Lily refused to take any advice.

'I'll find something! Got to have a decent door,' she declared, and flew into the woodland before Emily could offer more advice. Emily sympathised, remembering how she and Alice had always covered the doorway carefully, to make a private space. The single room of the tree-house held many memories, and she smiled to herself as she set about sweeping the winter's puddles and debris off the floor and through the doorway with her tail. She and Alice had decorated the woven branches that formed the walls, but Lily and Georgie didn't bother with such details.

It was not long before Lily returned, carrying a thick bundle of ivy strands with plenty of leaves still attached. Emily helped her to fasten them to the top of the door, where they hung down to the floor, making an effective screen. 'That'll do for now,' Lily said, after she had inspected it critically from outside and in. 'The bracken and heather are still too wet for beds. I'll leave that 'til Georgie comes. I wish they'd hurry up! It's so *boring* with just grown-ups.' Emily remembered it well! It had been her fierce longing for a friend that had brought about the meeting with Desmond and the English dragon family the year that Lily had hatched. But at least she had had Tom; life was more solitary for Lily, who was so much younger. No wonder she lost her temper so often!

She put a sympathetic wing round her young sister. 'Help me clear a few of those brambles from their camping place,' she said. 'Then we'll see if they've arrived at the cave. They'll probably land there first. I wonder how long Tom and Ollie will be.'

'They might not come at all,' Lily sighed as they flew down from the tree. '*I* wouldn't bother to come back here if I had the whole world to explore. Georgie says he's going to go with them next time they head off travelling. And I want to go too. I bet Dad won't let me! I'll sneak off in the middle of the night if he says no again. I HATE being the youngest!' She was swiping brambles more and more wildly with her spiked tail as she spoke. Emily sympathised, but knew that her parents would certainly not agree to Lily leaving home just yet. Her brightly shining gold scales and wings were too conspicuous, Emily thought - any Human who spotted her would be bound to try to capture and cage her. And she was so reckless; she always had been – even worse than Emily herself.

They had cleared a good-sized area for the travellers and were thinking about returning to the cave when a shout from above made them look up. Des was hovering just above the trees. 'They're nearly here!' he called. 'Come on!' He led the way in a fast swoop to the top of Ben's head, where the three of them watched and waved to the returning travellers, Lily dancing in excitement and huffing bursts of flame – a new accomplishment that she was still proud of and wanted to show off.

The ledge outside the cave, between Ben McIlwhinnie's boots, seemed very crowded as Ellen and Oliver, Alice and Georgie landed and folded their aching wings. It had been a long flight. Emily hugged Alice, delighted to see her best friend again, while Lily and Georgie – who seemed much less tired than his parents – danced round each other in delight. Georgie had grown, Emily thought, and was almost as big as Ollie, his deep orange colour a dramatic contrast to Lily's gold. She could imagine him travelling with Ollie and Tom if they would let him. Duncan and Gwen brought drinks for everyone, and the travellers gradually got their breath back and gazed around happily.

'It looks just the same!' Ellen said to Gwen, gazing down the Glen towards the woods and the loch. 'I always miss this place over the winter. It's lovely to be back.'

'Is our old camping ground still safe?' Oliver asked anxiously.

'Yes,' Emily reassured them. 'Lily and I were down there this morning. No Human footprints, no rubbish lying about. There's been no one in this bit of the Glen either.'

'We've been very lucky!' Duncan launched into an account of the three weeks of Human invasion on the castle site, making it sound rather more dangerous than it had actually been. Emily sighed. She had been looking forward to giving Alice an account of this herself. Luckily, Oliver and Ellen, who had always lived closer to Humans, seemed less concerned than her father, though they listened politely and sympathised.

'Why don't you stay here tonight?' Gwen suggested, after the welcome supper had been enjoyed and the evening was advancing. 'You must be tired, and there's plenty of room. I expect Des and Emily will be heading up the hill.'

'Alice can come with us,' Emily offered, looking forward to a longer and more private talk. 'Lily and Georgie won't want to be parted.' The two young dragons had flown down to the loch after supper, saying that Georgie, who had recovered from his flight remarkably quickly, wanted a swim; meaning some peace and quiet away from the grown-ups, Des thought, watching them go and remembering his own younger days.

Back at their own cave, a little later, Des, Emily and Alice sat by a small fire as the gloaming deepened and the moon rose over the mountains. After a while, Desmond retired to bed, leaving the friends to their talk. Alice smiled as he left. 'That was tactful of him!' she said fondly. 'You are SO lucky, Emily!' Emily stole a glance at her and was relieved to see that Alice was looking quite cheerful. Since she had settled down with Des in her own cave, she had wished that Alice too could find a mate of her own. Another reason for coming out of hiding, she thought. They needed to see if more dragons, like themselves, were living in secret. She and Des had found none in their travels, but perhaps Ollie and Tom would have some news when they returned. She started to tell Alice about the three weeks of Human invasion on the castle site, adding rather more detail than she had confessed to Duncan, and listened in turn to Alice's account of their winter further south. 'We had to move quite often,' Alice finished. 'I do miss that old castle of Angie's! That was a great winter, when we were all together and had somewhere safe to stay. It was a shock when we discovered the Humans had taken away the fence and knocked the house down.'

'Are the cellars still there?'

'We don't know. It would be much too dangerous to go and look. We've no idea where Angie, Maggie and Harold went. They just disappeared.'

'I hope they got away safely,' said Emily. 'Des still reckons Maggie's the best cook ever! Des and I have been keeping a look-out for caves that you could live in for the winter, but we haven't found one that looks safe enough. Humans seem to like caves and ruins as much as we do.' Glancing at Alice, she realised that her friend was almost asleep, and remembered how long their flight had been. 'Come and sleep in the cave,' she said. 'It's getting chilly out here.' She showed Alice the soft heather bed that had been dried specially for her and tiptoed through the cave to join Des without waking him.

In the middle of the night she woke and sat up, startled. There seemed to be a strange scrabbling noise just outside the cave. Was some animal trying to get in? If so, it was quite a big one, and how on earth had it got up to the ledge? Should she wake Des? No, whatever it was, she'd sort it out herself! She crept round Des, careful not to tread on his tail, past Alice, curled up fast asleep, and paused just inside the entrance to listen again. Nothing – she must have been dreaming. No – there it was again! She stepped cautiously outside and almost tripped over a heap of something that had *certainly* not been there earlier.

The heap stirred, and a voice said, through a vast yawn, 'Sorry, Em! It's only me and Ollie. Go back to bed. See you in the morning. Not too early…OK…?' The voice tailed off into another yawn.

Tom! Typical!!

She crept back to bed.

2

Fortunately, everyone woke late the following morning, but they were all alerted to the midnight visitor by Des's yell as he fell over Tom on his way out of the cave. Ollie, looking bleary-eyed, flew up from the lower ledge where he had been sleeping, and the noisy greeting of the five dragons irritated the ravens enough for the male to fly at them threateningly, until a fiery huff from Des sent him wheeling into the gorge. Another huff lit a fire below the cave, and the five of them gathered close to it while Des brewed some nettle tea. 'If you two hang your tails over the edge, there'll be more room!' said Emily as she tripped over Ollie's on her way up to the cave for some emergency breakfast. Alice was assuring Ollie that their parents were fine after their long flight, and about to set up the summer camp as usual.

'Why didn't you go to Ben's cave, or the camp?' she asked.

'There's a reason,' said Ollie. 'But let's swap travellers' tales first. Where have you two been?' He looked from Des to Emily, who took it in turns to describe their latest explorations, admitting that they had spent the worst of the winter in and around their cave, and more recently monitoring the Human camp down the valley. The last account interested Tom and Ollie the most. Des's travels seemed tame these days, compared to their own. Then Alice reported on their family base in a deep forest area further south, and their avoidance of Humans. 'We keep looking for some old ruin, like Angie's castle,' she admitted, 'but found nothing as safe as that place. And no sign of Angie and the others. It's getting more and more difficult to keep hidden. The Humans get everywhere! Georgie's fed up with it. He wants to go travelling with you two.' She sighed wistfully.

'Your turn!' Des challenged Ollie. 'Where have you two been?'

'West coast,' said Ollie, but Tom broke in eagerly. 'We've been exploring islands! And some amazing rocky cliffs. We did find a few caves, but only to shelter or hide in – nothing good enough to spend the winter, or make a proper home, like yours. Not that we were looking for anything like that, of course.'

'Well you should have been!' Alice interrupted. 'It's the thing we need most! A permanent place for Mum and Dad to live, so they don't have to keep on the move all the time. Emily and Des have been searching, so you should too!'

'Well, no luck on this trip,' Ollie admitted. 'We flew over one big island with jagged black mountains which might be worth looking at again, but snow was on its way, so we didn't stop. There were plenty of Humans on the islands, but we managed to avoid them, I think. We met up with a few of your Bonxies, Des. They said there were even *more* Humans around in summer. They're a plague! And they do seem to haunt the coasts, which is the most likely place for caves.'

Tom took up the story. 'But then we made the biggest discovery of the whole expedition,' he said eagerly. 'Time to show them, Ollie?'

'I reckon so.' Ollie leaned perilously over the edge and sent two huffs of white smoke down to the gorge below. A few moments later Alice and Emily gasped and Des rose up from the ledge in astonishment. A large bronze-coloured dragon, with spikes and wings of deep gold appeared from below, hovered for a moment in front of Des, and then, as Des nodded his agreement, landed carefully between Tom and Ollie, who moved aside a little to make room.

'Alice, Emily, Des, meet Seamus,' said Ollie. 'We met him on the West coast a week ago. He's flown all the way from the west of Ireland to look for us!'

There was a stunned silence. The new dragon bowed his head, formally.

'To look for *us*?' Des echoed, mystified, but Emily instantly understood. 'Edward and George!' she cried. 'They met dragons in Ireland. I saw them, sitting around a fire. But that was years ago, and I only heard a few times after that. Nothing for ages.'

The stranger was gazing at her intently. 'You are a Seer?' he asked, and when she nodded, added, 'I have only met two dragons with the gift before.'

'Old George?'

'And one other.' But this did not interest Emily at the moment.

'You've seen George?' she demanded. 'And Edward – my grandfather? I still miss them. I loved them both. Do you know where they are? Are they still alive?' Questions poured from her, and she was almost sobbing in her eagerness. Alice touched her talon. 'Sssh! Let him tell us, Emily,' she said gently. Des nodded in agreement and put a wing round Emily as they all gazed at the stranger.

Seamus took a deep breath. 'George and Edward are both dead now,' he said sadly, wanting to get this news over as soon as possible. Des's wing tightened round Emily as she gave a sob. 'They lived with us for several months, after they arrived from Wales. Ollie here said you were with them when they left?' Des and Emily both nodded. 'They found my family quite quickly, mainly because my mother is a Seer like you, and she and George made contact. There was a group of six of us, so we obviously made them welcome. Like you, we often feel isolated and alone. It was good to have news of dragons from across the sea. Your Edward was a fine teller of tales!' He looked round his listeners, noting their fond smiles of reminiscence as they also remembered Edward telling stories round the fire in the gloaming. 'We heard about the death of his wife, and the family he left behind. You people, of course! He described you all – though I hardly recognised Tom as the wee blue dragon he talked about!' Tom cringed in embarrassment as Ollie sniggered and patted him on the head. 'One thing interested us greatly,' Seamus continued. 'He said you had a golden baby. Pure gold! She sounds like a dragon from legend, and we could hardly believe it. Is she here? Will I be able to meet her?'

'Oh yes, she's not likely to stay hidden when she hears we have a visitor!' said Des. 'She lives down the Glen with her Mum and Dad. They have a much bigger cave. Gwen is a Seer too. They'll all want to meet you.'

'But PLEASE don't make Lily feel special!' Tom urged. 'She's too full of herself without that. You wait! That's why me and Ollie go travelling – to get away from her.'

'She's not that bad!' Emily protested. 'She'll be a lot better now Georgie's back. She gets bored. It's not surprising, really. Tell us more about Edward and George,' she pleaded.

'They stayed with us for many weeks,' Seamus continued. 'They met some of our friendly Humans.'

'What?' Des exclaimed. Ollie and Tom both nodded – they had already heard the story.

'I saw them!' Emily said, remembering. 'In a Call from George. Two Humans and several dragons, sharing a talk round the fire. We once met friendly Humans too, but it was a long time ago. How did you meet yours?'

'But tell us about George and Edward first,' Alice insisted, and Emily subsided.

'They stayed with us until the following spring,' Seamus continued. 'Then I took them travelling around Ireland, and we met a few other dragons, who welcomed us, and at every place they told of your groups, in Scotland and England. And there were a few more friendly Humans too, and we learnt a lot from them. As summer drew to a close they planned to fly back to Scotland to tell you of all they had learnt, but George was getting weaker. He gradually lost the gift of the Call over his time with us and knew his death was near. The night before he died, he made me promise that I would look after Edward for the rest of his life, and when I was free, that I should search for you. When we had sent George to his rest, Edward and I travelled back to my home, where he lived with my family, much loved, until he died last year. We miss him, and not just for his stories. We treasure the memory of both of them. Your two wise old dragons fulfilled their last quest with honour, and I pledged to continue it as well as I could. So, I am very glad to have found you. It's a good start!'

There was silence round the fire as Seamus finished his story. They were all solemn, and tears rolled unchecked down Emily's nose. 'Thank you,' said Alice quietly. 'It's good to know the end of their story. And thank you for your care of them. You were very kind.'

'So were they!' said Seamus, smiling and trying for a more cheerful note. 'A Seer and a Storyteller; great gifts to travel with, and a blessing when they arrive in your midst!'

'The parents will want the story,' said Ollie. 'We'll take you to meet them later. But first, how about food? The three of us need feeding up after our travels! How are your stocks?'

'Pretty depleted, after the winter,' Des admitted, 'but we'll find you something.' He got up to fly back to the cave, but Ollie stopped him.

'Good thing we brought a contribution then!' he said, and he and Tom dropped down to the floor of the gorge and returned in triumph with four fat grouse. 'There are dozens of these on the high moor over there,' he added, waving a wing. 'Too stupid to escape and almost too fat to fly. Stoke up the fire and let's get plucking!'

In spite of Emily's eagerness to hear more about the 'friendly Humans', everyone agreed that they should postpone this discussion until Seamus had met the rest of the family and told again the news of George and Edward. Humans, friendly or otherwise, was not a subject that Duncan would want to hear about, and it had to be handled carefully. By the time the late breakfast of well-roasted grouse was finished, the morning was almost over, and they discovered that Ellen and Oliver had flown to the small loch to re-establish their camp site. When they had recovered from the shock of the stranger, Gwen and Duncan flew over with him so that the tale of Edward and George could be told to all of them together. Lily, fascinated by this new dragon, and enjoying his obvious admiration, elected to go with them, leaving Georgie to join Tom and Ollie down at the loch. Emily and Alice sat on a rock at the edge of the water and watched as the boys held a high-dive competition and Des flew to join in. 'He's still pretty good at it,' Emily admitted watching him dive as fast as the younger dragons. 'But there's not much chance of any fishing after that!'

'Where are the otters?' Alice asked. 'Surely they haven't been scared away?'

'I don't know. Wattie often takes his new mate down the burn to the river. There won't be any cubs just yet this year, so I expect she's exploring while she can. Do you remember how Des used to take them flying?' They chuckled, remembering summers past, then Emily reverted to her main preoccupation. 'We must get back up the hill in time to ask Seamus about their friendly Humans,' she said. 'I have a feeling this is most important. We can't tell the parents, of course – not yet anyway. And I want to show him where our Humans were digging. He might know what they were doing. It's obvious that they have more dealings with Humans over in Ireland. And they haven't ended up in cages, so it can't be as dangerous as we think. I wish they'd hurry up and finish their diving competition!'

'I don't think Seamus is in any hurry to leave,' Alice reminded her. 'Be patient!' She smiled fondly, knowing quite well that patience was not Emily's strong point. Alice had always been more sensible as a young dragon, and not always approving when Emily took reckless risks with Humans, but these days they didn't fall out about it.

They looked up as they heard beating wings, and Lily and Seamus appeared and glided down to join them. Lily was obviously enjoying showing their visitor around, Emily thought, which might explain why Georgie seemed to be sulking. He stayed in the middle of the loch, while the others shook the water from their wings and flew over to the bank, but then followed them, obviously to make sure he didn't miss anything. He settled at the edge of the group and pointedly ignored Lily. Des caught Emily's eye and winked.

'I have never seen such a fine cave,' Seamus was saying. 'We have some in Ireland, but they are too often visited by Humans. Obviously, your Mountain Giant has protected it well. Gwen and Duncan have invited me to stay with them. They say there's plenty of room, more than you have up the mountain. It would be good to stay for a few days, if you agree.' He looked round the group, noting smiles and nods. 'Good. I can help with some hunting and fishing, as you say your stocks are low. I know what it's like at the end of winter. I expect your weather is harsh, up here.'

'We definitely want you to stay. There's lots more we want to learn about dragons in Ireland,' said Emily. She was feeling a bit frustrated. If her parents – and Lily – were going to monopolise Seamus, how would she *ever* learn about Irish Humans? Des read her mind, as he so often did.

'Let's take Seamus to see the local sights after supper,' he said. 'Evening's a good time.'

'Ellen says we're all to go to the camp for supper,' Lily announced. 'She's started cooking already, and Mum and Dad are helping. Early supper, she said, so that the travellers can get a decent night's sleep.' Emily saw her chances diminish and realised she would have to wait.

'Tomorrow evening, then,' said Des. 'I'm going back to our cave to fetch some Firewater. Time for a celebration! Come on, Em, we can look out some food to add to the supper while we're there.' As they left, Emily glanced back and saw Tom and Ollie invite Seamus in for a swim, leaving Lily and Georgie sitting at opposite ends of the bank. Lily had her nose in the air. She looked at Des and laughed. 'I wonder who'll crumble first,' she said.

'Georgie,' said Des. 'No contest!'

3

'I *have* seen this sort of thing before,' Seamus said thoughtfully, surveying the square diggings at the castle site. Emily and Des had finally found a time to take him on a recce without including Georgie and Lily, who were less reliable with secrets. 'I was told by a

Human that it's where they're digging to find out about Humans from the past. Sometimes they dig up bones and take them away.'

'Makes me glad we burn our bodies,' Des remarked. 'I wouldn't like to think of them digging *us* up!' He stopped, fearing he had revived Emily's sadness over George and Edward, but she was too absorbed in Seamus's information. Tom and Ollie, who had joined them, were searching along the edge of the site in the hope of finding some Human relic that Des and Emily had missed.

'I have never seen such a tidy place where Humans have been,' Alice remarked. 'Me and my family have sometimes seen those tent places that we read about, Emily, but never one left as clean as this.'

'Do you think they might have been *'friendly Humans'* like yours, Seamus?' Emily asked hopefully. 'I thought they didn't sound dangerous when I heard them singing round the fire, but Des wouldn't let me go down to find out.'

'How many were there?'

'Lots.'

'Then he was probably right. You must be sure that *no one* will pose a danger before venturing to make contact. The more there are, the greater the risk.'

Des smirked triumphantly at Emily, who ignored him.

'I just have a feeling they were all right,' she continued, speaking to Seamus. 'We met four Human children years ago, and we're sure they never told anyone about us. They promised, and Alice and I believed them. Even Ollie did in the end. Des didn't, but he was wrong. He often is, though he never admits it.' She glared at Des, but he just grinned and huffed her a kiss.

'Young Humans are different,' Ollie had joined them. 'It's the grown-ups you can't trust.'

'Not all grown-up Humans are like the ones that captured you.' Seamus had heard Ollie's story of his kidnap and caging. 'But you have to be sure. As Alice says, it's a good sign if they leave no rubbish behind. The ones who explore hills and mountains and love the wild creatures are most likely to be safe. The two your grandparents met were good friends to our family. They helped us in many ways, and always warned us if there was any danger of discovery. But they agreed with us that we had to keep ourselves secret. They couldn't solve the problem that all dragons face – that we need to stay in hiding, and sometimes that means moving from place to place. You are lucky that you have found somewhere to live settled secret lives, but it may not last. These Humans might come again. They might explore further and find your cave. If they do, they'll certainly enter it. As you've learnt on your travels, Ollie – Humans can't resist exploring caves and ruins. You may have to leave in a hurry.'

'We could stand and fight!' Ollie declared, and Tom nodded agreement. 'Lure them in and then attack! They can't breathe fire. If those Humans hadn't surprised me years ago, I'd have burnt them to ashes!'

'Humans have fire too, and to kill one would be the most dangerous thing you could possibly do,' Seamus said soberly. 'We have been very lucky with the help our Human friends have given us in Ireland. It would be worth making contact with one or two up here if you ever have the chance. You wear a Human token, I think,' he added, turning to Emily. 'Was it given by one of the children you met?'

Emily looped her silver pendant on the end of a talon and showed it to him. 'Alice and I used to wear coloured bobbles that the children gave us, but mine broke and got lost. This was a gift from my Gran just before she died. She was given it by a friendly Human girl, who was riding a pony on the moors.' Seamus nodded, recognising the right kind of Human. 'But she gave me a Quest as well – *to bring about an understanding between the few dragons that remain and the Humans who will cherish them* - that's exactly what she said to me the night she died. I recited it to myself that night before I went to sleep and lots of times since, so that I can never forget. But I haven't done much about it. I'm very much afraid I've failed her.'

Seamus smiled. 'There's time yet!' he said. 'Don't give up hope. But the problem we face is that there are so few of us, and so many Humans. And not nearly enough of the right kind!'

'It sounds as though Ireland might be a better bet. More dragons and nicer Humans,' said Ollie. 'Tom and I are thinking of taking a trip over there. Why don't we all go?'

'It's not a good idea to travel in a big group,' said Des.

'Honestly!' Tom rolled his eyes. 'Nobody would think you were a Traveller! Where's your spirit of adventure gone?'

'I'm a settled Dragon with responsibilities now!' Des declared.

'No, you're not!' said Emily. 'I refuse to be a responsibility! I agree with Ollie and Tom. I think we should all go to Ireland. Don't you, Alice?'

Alice hesitated. 'It would be lovely, but it would be rather hard on the parents if we *all* went. And Georgie seems to think you and Tom have agreed to take him on your next trip, Ollie.'

'We didn't exactly *agree*!' Ollie said.

'I think we said *'sometime'*. And he needs some practise trips first, not a long journey over the sea,' Tom protested, remembering the many training flights he had been forced to undertake in his own younger days.

'And what about Lily?' Alice added. 'I can't see her letting a mass trip to Ireland happen without a fight!' Tom shuddered at the thought.

'Do you have to head straight back to Ireland?' Des asked Seamus. He had decided to take the lead on the decision-making before Tom and Ollie got carried away. 'Why don't you stay for a month or so? The lads could take Georgie for a few practise flights, and even Lily might be able to try. All right, Tom, not with you; Em and I could take her! I'd like to go to Ireland myself, but we've the whole summer before us. Now shut up, all of you! Seamus, what do *you* think?'

Seamus smiled round at the hopeful faces. 'I *would* like to stay a little longer, if you think your families would agree. As I said, I can help with the hunting! It would be better if I came with you when you travel to Ireland - it's a big place, and not much of it is safe. Emily, you and Gwen are Seers; could you send a Call to my mother to let her know that I've found you and will be staying for a while?'

'Of course we will!'

'That's settled then,' said Des. 'Let's go and tell the parents that you've joined the family. They're good at adopting people. Look at me!'

'And *most* of the time we haven't regretted it!' Emily declared.

LISA

1

Finn and Lisa met Matthew off the Manchester train a week before the beginning of term. He was heavily laden, with a rucksack full of camping gear, a large hold-all with clothes and books for the summer term, his computer bag, binoculars and – to Lisa's secret satisfaction – a guitar case. Between them, they hauled it all from Glasgow Central Station to Finn's flat, where they would spend the night before heading north on what Lisa termed their Dragon Quest. The loan of the car had caused complications, but it had been arranged that Steve would collect it in Glasgow on their return, leaving Finn in his flat to start the term, and Lisa and Matthew to collect their belongings and travel on to Edinburgh by train. After a night in the flat – fortunately vacated by Finn's flatmates – they could make an early start.

'I owe Steve big-time for this!' Finn pointed out as they climbed the stairs to the second floor. 'I hate to think what it'll cost me!'

'We'll all chip in for a good bottle of Scotch on the way back,' Lisa promised as they fought their way into the hallway with the luggage.

'Nice flat,' said Matthew, when they had dumped his belongings and got their breath back. 'Hall's OK, but I'm looking forward to getting a flat for next year. Did you know your flatmates before you moved in?'

'No. But it worked out well – we all get on. One guy's moved his girl-friend in more or less permanently, so it's a bit more crowded than it was. She's OK. Tends to hog the bathroom, though.'

'And she doesn't do your washing for you?' Lisa queried, sarcastically. 'What a shame!'

'We'll ring for a take-away, then we can take a look at your maps,' Finn said, ignoring her. 'Pizza? Indian?'

They settled for pizza. 'Fewer drips on the maps,' Lisa remarked with her mouth full, spreading her detailed Ordinance Survey map on the kitchen table alongside Finn's road atlas. She traced the road route with her finger, and she and Matthew agreed on the turning that led to their dig site. 'We need to decide where to leave the car. I don't think we can risk the hostel, after what Sophie said about the old Factor. He certainly seemed a bit hostile.'

'I'd rather not leave it in a lay-by on the main road,' said Finn. 'There must be somewhere safe up this unmarked one. And it'll shorten the walk to the site as well. After all, you've done that bit, as far as the old castle marked here. Better to explore new areas. Which valley did you say looked interesting?'

'This one,' Matthew traced the line of the burn from the main valley. 'Up to this loch here. We could camp there – looks like a bit of flat ground beside it. Then we could carry on and have a look at that weird hill with the bald head....'

Finn looked baffled. 'Is this another of Lisa's tall stories?'

'Wait 'til you see it!' Lisa promised. 'Then if we have time, there looks to be a decent sized gorge further up, with a waterfall. It all looks interesting. Up above on the other side it seems to be high moorland – full of grouse probably. Boring. And we're more likely to run into the Factor with his grumpy Keep Out face.'

'Who does the land belong to?'

'Some rich foreigner, according to Dave Andrews. It isn't the shooting season, so he won't be there,' Lisa said confidently.

'That all sounds fine – but what about the car?' They stared at the map.

'I think there's a sort of disused quarry site on the way up that road,' Matthew said thoughtfully. 'It was well above the last of the houses, about half way on the left as you drive up. I noticed it when we were heading home. It just looked like an open space by the road – not an entrance or anything. You were on the other side of the bus, Lisa, so you probably didn't notice it. I can't see it marked though. Oh yes, this might be it!' He pointed to a small marked semi-circle adjoining the road. 'I think that's about the right place.'

'OK, suppose we just drive slowly up the road and look-out for it,' said Finn. 'With luck we'll get at least half way before we have to start walking. Don't want to slog the whole length of it unless we have to. But I definitely need somewhere safe for the old crate, or it'll cost me a lot more than a bottle of Scotch! We need to be back to retrieve it by next weekend.'

'Anyway, that should give us plenty of time for a dragon-hunt up the valley,' Lisa declared happily. Finn looked across at Matthew and shook his head in mock despair.

'I'll settle for some decent exploring.'

'And I'll settle for another look at those eagles. We might find their nest further up.'

'Well, we'll see won't we!' Lisa got up. 'I'm for an early night, then we can start at the crack of dawn. Mustn't waste a minute so don't be late! Night!' She blew a kiss in the direction of both of them and disappeared into the room across the passage, belonging to an absent flat-mate.

The two boys, united for once, looked at each other. 'She's going to be dreadfully disappointed, isn't she?' Matthew said sadly.

'Yes. But then she'll think up another plan. She never gives up!'

'I've noticed!' Matthew said dryly. 'We'll just have to humour her. I think I'll turn in too – that room, yeah?' He turned at the door. 'Thanks for letting me come, by the way.'

'Didn't have much choice,' Finn said ruefully to himself as he switched off the lights and headed for his own bed.

2

Lisa had set an early alarm and enjoyed a last leisurely shower before she bullied the boys out of bed. To make amends, she cooked bacon rolls and brewed decent coffee, and once they were well fed, her companions woke up properly and helped with the packing. They left the flat tidy for Finn's friends, who would probably be back before them, made a neat pile of Matthew's luggage ready for collection on their return and loaded the car. Once they were clear of the suburbs of Glasgow, they made good time. The day was bright, and fortunately the low sun was behind them as they headed north into the Highlands, with music playing through the elderly speakers. Lisa sang along to Queen, hoping that Matthew would join in, but he didn't.

'Still quite a bit of snow,' Finn remarked some time later, looking around as the mountains on either side rose steadily. Matthew had offered to drive for a while to allow him a share of the view, and Finn had agreed, though he had taken Lisa's seat in the front in order to keep a closer eye on him. As he had remarked, the old crate was temperamental, and had controls in odd places. Matthew had switched on the wipers instead of the indicators more than once.

'Less than when we were here,' Lisa answered. 'I checked the forecast again. It's looking good.'

'So why is it starting to drizzle?' Finn queried. Matthew hit the indicator instead of the wipers this time and swore as Lisa giggled. She had the map and was navigating from the back seat. 'How much further to your bumpy turning? Do we need a loo break?'

'Let's stop at that place we went to with the bus,' Lisa suggested. 'It's not much further up the road. We can have an early lunch. They did decent soup. We could see if they've got any of that fantastic gingerbread to take with us.'

'Their chocolate brownies were good too.'

'I'm warming to this trip,' said Finn. 'We can switch drivers there,' he added. 'I'll nurse the crate over the road up the valley.'

A little over an hour later, with their purchases carefully balanced on the back-seat luggage, they were driving slowly, keeping a sharp look-out for the hidden turning. 'There!' said Lisa and Matthew, almost together, and Finn braked and swung the car into the narrow road. 'I see what you mean!' he said, as it became even narrower and more rutted. 'I'm glad Steve can't see us! What happens if we meet something?'

'We hope there's no hidden ditch in the verge,' said Matthew. 'I don't think that parking place is much further. We passed all the house gates and that last farmyard a few miles back. Go slowly.'

'Not much chance of anything else!' said Finn, swerving the car to avoid a particularly large pothole.

They rounded a few more corners, then Matthew said, 'I think that might be it up ahead.' Sure enough, they could see a small expanse of weedy ground, bounded by a semi-circle of vertical rock walls with bushes growing at the base and in the crevices. 'It does look like a small quarry,' Finn said. 'I reckon the car will be safe enough here. There's no 'Keep Out' notice. Better not park too close to those rock walls though. You can see where stones have fallen.' He pulled up between two of the larger bushes and they climbed out. Lisa took a deep breath and stretched her arms wide.

'Perfect!' she said. 'Rain's stopped, sun's about to shine. Plenty of time to get to the hostel place before dark. We might even make it to the dig site.'

Matthew shook his head. 'I don't think we'll get that far today. It must be six or seven miles to the hostel, and same again to the dig.'

'And uphill,' Finn added, hoisting his rucksack. 'Let's get going. Sure we've got everything?'

'Yes, including gingerbread!' said Lisa. 'Let's go!'

They set a steady pace, following the road and gazing about them as they walked. The late spring temperature, sun alternating with cloud, was perfect for hiking, though they knew the nights would be cold, probably frosty. In the three weeks since the end of the dig, new green fronds of bracken and whin had appeared and on the slopes above them Lisa spotted a small herd of deer with a couple of new-born fawns, still staggery on their legs. Matthew had been forbidden his binoculars until they had a scheduled stop, but they all agreed this was a special case, and took turns watching the tiny creatures nose at the grasses in imitation of their elders. This time it was Finn who urged them on, and reluctantly Lisa returned the binoculars to Matthew and agreed. 'There'll be plenty more, I expect,' he sympathised, packing them carefully into their case. They drank some water, then continued up the hill, munching cereal bars as they walked.

The sun was sinking as they crested the last rise and looked down into the dip where the old hostel stood. 'Is that a small tree sprouting from the roof?' Finn asked. 'What a wreck of a place! Did your lot actually *stay* there?'

'Just for one night,' said Lisa. 'It's primitive. But it would save pitching the tents if we could find a way in.'

Unfortunately, when they arrived at the front door it was obvious that the place was more secure than it looked. The heavy door was locked fast, and they failed to find a window that they could open. But round the back, against the hillside, they came across a neat stack of firewood, which might have been left specially for them. 'We won't need much,' said Matthew as they each took an armful. 'We can cook on the Trangia, but a fire will be great. There's a sheltered place round the side of the hostel; we can pitch the tents there. You can see where other folk have had a fire. Ages ago, but there's still a ring of stones.'

'Better get started then,' Finn said. 'The light's fading pretty fast.'

'You're great with fires, Finn,' Lisa said. 'I'll put up your tent while you get it going.' She and Matthew pitched the three small tents in a semi-circle round the fireplace, unrolled sleeping bags inside and then unpacked the little camping stove, balancing it on a large flat rock. Finn's fire was burning steadily by the time they had finished. They sat close to it, eating the home-made hot-pot that Lisa had brought in a sealed container to heat on the stove, and finishing with fruit, hot chocolate and brownies. 'That was probably our best meal,' Matthew said appreciatively. 'I suspect it's downhill from here.' He found a torch and took the empty pan down to the burn, bringing it back clean and filled with water to warm on the dying embers of the fire.

'Hot water for a wash!' Lisa remarked. 'This is luxury!'

'I'm for bed,' said Finn. 'I can live with grubby. It's been a long day, considering we were dragged out of bed at dawn.' Lisa made a face at him as he passed on the way to his tent, adding, 'And if anyone hears flapping wings in the night, don't wake me!' He switched on his torch in the tent, and his weirdly shaped shadow waved wildly as he struggled out of the top layers of clothing and wriggled into his sleeping bag.

Lisa and Matthew sat on by the fire, waiting for their water to heat. An owl hooted close by, and there was an answering call from across the burn. 'Tawnies,' Matthew said quietly. 'Something splashed away when I was getting the water, but I couldn't see what it was. Smaller than a deer. Probably not a dragon either.'

'The dragons will be further up the glen,' Lisa said seriously. 'They wouldn't come as far down as this.' She caught Matthew's grin in the light of the fire and tilted her chin haughtily. 'All right, fine! I know you're not taking this quest seriously, and neither is Finn, but you wait 'til we get to the REAL wild country! I'll show you both!'

Matthew smiled as he lifted the pan carefully off the fire. 'I'll be satisfied with the eagles. And there might be ospreys by that big loch. Or otters – or both. It's too cloudy for a moon tonight, or I might be tempted to go for a walk and look for those owls. Let's turn in. If we get an early start, we should reach the loch tomorrow. Here - have first dip in the hot water.'

3

The sun woke them early, but all three had managed a decent night's sleep, undisturbed by wings, weather or wild beasts, as Finn remarked as he crawled from his tent. They put on water for tea and fried sausages on the stove, wedging them in flattened morning rolls. Matthew went down to the burn to wash the mugs and pan, and they rolled up their tents and bedding and repacked their rucksacks. Somehow things never fitted as neatly, second-time around. It was a cloudless morning as they set off up the track with the wind behind them, blowing up the valley. They intended to take the 'short cut' to the castle site. This proved slower going, as the ground was marshy in places, but, as Lisa remarked, it was more interesting than sticking to the track.

They were beginning to think hungrily of lunch by noon when the castle mound came into sight. The stones on the top would provide better seats than damp heather, so they carried on, pausing first to inspect what remained of their trenches and point out to Finn the main features of the dig camp. From the top, the paler patches where their tents had been, the blackened bonfire circle and the outlines of the trenches were laid out clearly, and Matthew explained some of their findings.

'It seems an odd place to build a castle!' said Finn. 'There's nothing for miles!'

'It was more of a defensive tower than a castle, we think,' Matthew said. 'I suppose it must have been a strategic point in the division of the clan lands. It's quite a decent viewpoint, up and down and sideways.'

'It was definitely destroyed by fire,' Lisa added. 'Probably in the thirteenth century. The settlement we excavated seems to have been abandoned about the same time. It wasn't a very important dig, but it was fun, wasn't it, Matt? I'd love to try one of the big ones, like the Orkney dig that Sophie is doing in the summer. I'm definitely getting keener on archaeology.' They munched cheese rolls, crisps and apples as they gazed down at the dig.

'It looks as though something's been scrabbling at the edge of that trench.' Matthew pointed. 'Could be any number of creatures, I suppose – rabbits, foxes, hares....' He was getting his binoculars out as he spoke. 'There are some rather odd footprints.'

'Where, where?' Lisa snatched at the binoculars, pulling him sideways in the process. He extricated himself from the carrying strap with difficulty, but Lisa seemed oblivious to his efforts and Finn's sniggers. 'Oh yes, I see. They look like the marks of big talons. Honestly!' she added, as the boys groaned. 'You look!' She passed the binoculars back to Matthew, who had a good look before passing them to Finn. 'Well?' she demanded impatiently.

'I agree something's been digging around down there,' Finn admitted. 'But it could be anything. I certainly can't see big talon prints. Can you?' he asked Matthew.

'There's something a bit talon-shaped,' Matthew admitted, taking another look. 'I suspect an eagle's come down, after prey. We get the best view from up here. I don't think it's worth going back down for a closer look. Whatever it was, it's not there now.' He glanced at Lisa, noting the familiar frown. 'OK, if you want to think it was one of your dragons, we'll keep looking. Let's head up towards the loch.'

'Don't encourage her!' Finn grumbled. 'Can I have a squint at this peculiar mountain before we go? Oh yes, I see what you mean about the bald head!' He chuckled and passed the binoculars back as the others began to repack their rucksacks, stowing the empty wrappings carefully in a side pocket. They scrambled down the mound and, skirting the lochan, began to pick a route close to the burn.

It was slow going. There was no sign of a proper path, though there were faint suggestions of deer tracks branching out from the burn. 'Good thing it isn't misty,' Finn remarked. 'It's not easy to keep close to the burn, and that's our only guide to this loch on the map.' They scrambled through bracken and heather, pausing frequently to take a breather and to look round at the stunning scenery. The pair of eagles that Matthew had noted on his earlier visit, circled lazily in the sky above them, and they startled several grouse, which whirred away noisily, flying low. There were more deer grazing on the slopes above them, half- hidden in heather and too far away to see clearly.

After more than an hour of slow tramping in a landscape that seemed unchanging, Matthew opened the map again, and they gathered round to study it. They could still see the castle mound in the distance behind them, which as Finn remarked, was *some* comfort, as they now seemed to be in the middle of nowhere. He was threatening to lose faith in this expedition, Lisa thought, hoping that the loch would come into sight soon. The afternoon was wearing on with a bank of cloud edging ominously nearer the sun. Fortunately, Matthew still seemed to share her faith that they were on track. He traced the line of the burn on the map and looked about him.

'We've moved away from the stream, but you can see the line of it over there,' he said. 'I can just about hear it too. There's a dip in the ridge ahead – I bet that's where it flows down. I reckon we're not far from the bottom end of the loch. If we can get over that ridge we should be able to see it. Let's head straight up.'

'Not easy to do *straight* in this country,' Finn grumbled, 'but I suppose it's our best bet. It doesn't look far, but I bet it's further than you think.' He was right. It was tiring picking their way through high bracken, but they struggled on, climbing steadily and trying to keep an even pace. As always, the crest of the ridge appeared to be receding, but finally, as even Lisa was beginning to give up hope, Matthew in the lead reached the top and gave a yell of triumph. He turned, beaming, and the other two picked up the pace and joined him.

'Wow!' panted Lisa as the view opened out in front of her. Matthew led the way to a large rock and they sat in a row, catching their breath and gazing up the glen. Finn opened a side pocket in his rucksack and passed round water and chocolate. In the westering sun, the glen shone with a golden light. The nearest edge of the loch was perhaps half a mile away, with the long narrow length of it stretching away towards the strange shaped hill and the higher mountains beyond. At the far end were more trees than they expected, a patch of what appeared to be mixed woodland, some of the trees showing a haze of new green. They could see large boulders and clumps of bulrushes around the edge of the water. The burn that they had followed emerged out of the loch to their right, and they heard the tumble of water as it flowed over the gap in the ridge and down the valley. Matthew passed the binoculars around, and they all swept the landscape slowly. 'Couple of deer over there,' said Finn. 'Smaller ones – not the reds. Moving into the trees.'

Matthew gazed down at the loch. 'Something moving on the water,' he said, reaching for the binoculars. 'I do believe it's a pair of Divers! Wow! First I've ever seen, but you can't mistake the shape. I can't see which breed from this distance. One's gone down. I hope we don't frighten them off when we get nearer.'

'Let's see if that patch of green halfway up will do for the tents,' said Finn, fastening his rucksack. 'It might be too soggy. OK to carry on?' He seemed to have got over his pessimism, which was a relief, Matthew thought as he brought up the rear.

Fifteen minutes of walking and scrambling brought them to the edge of the loch, and they moved along the bank as quietly as they could, keeping a keen look-out for Matthew's divers, which seemed to have disappeared. A pair of coots near the bank took no notice of them but a moorhen scuttered away across the surface. Suddenly Matthew stopped dead and clutched Lisa's arm. 'Otter!' he breathed, pointing. A round dark shape had appeared on the surface near the far bank. As they watched, not daring to move, a humped back appeared and the head vanished. 'Fantastic!' whispered Lisa. 'You said there might be otters, but I didn't dare believe you.'

'I think that's another,' said Finn as a head appeared again, a good deal further away.

'Might be the same one. They move fast under water. No, you're right, there *are* two. We MUST find a camping place by the water. It's a great chance to watch them at close quarters. They've probably never seen humans up here, so they shouldn't be too wary.'

'Here's hoping the green bit's OK then,' said Finn, setting off again. Lisa mimed crossed fingers and grinned happily at Matthew as they followed.

Unnoticed behind them, the otter resurfaced and gazed after them suspiciously. It was joined by the second one. It was fortunate that the three students, tramping steadily towards the green patch, were also facing away from the largest rock on the far bank; behind it, a long blue nose, breathing faint puffs of almost transparent smoke, was just visible, and one sharp eye was watching.

The green patch was disappointing; too damp, almost marshy, and no good for tents. They carried on close to the shore. Matthew was almost in despair until they came upon a small semi-circle of sandy ground with a tiny stream running down one edge into the loch. It was soft and dry, and just big enough for the three tents and a fire-place. 'Not much spare space,' Finn remarked, after Lisa and Matthew, in relief, had both pronounced it perfect. 'Tents will be packed together. Let's hope nobody snores! No firewood either,' he added.

'There's probably lots of dead wood under the trees over there,' Lisa said, dumping her rucksack. 'Let's put the tents up, then go and see. It won't be dusk for an hour or so.'

'Get the tents out of your bags and I'll put them up, if you two want to go and find some,' Finn offered. 'I know you're dying to explore.'

'Oh thanks, Finn! You're a star!' Lisa declared, giving him a quick hug. 'Come on, Matt.'

'Hang on!' Finn called as they were about to set off. 'Leave the binoculars! That way you'll come straight back with the wood!'

'Fair point!' Matthew acknowledged with a grin, turning and dumping them on top of his rucksack. 'Cheers!' He sprinted to catch up with Lisa, who was heading for the top of the loch on her way to the wood. She beamed as he came alongside.

'Isn't it just *perfect*!' she said quietly as they passed under the first of the trees. 'It feels as though we're the first people ever to come here. This wood is *old* and nothing like the planted stretches of fir trees you usually find. That oak has stood here for years and years, all twisted and thick and spreading. And that's rowan, just coming into leaf. And silver birch. Birds high up – I can hear them twittering.'

'Tits, I think,' Matthew said, gazing up through the branches. 'I can't see them though. There's a few bits of fallen wood over there. Better not get side-tracked, or Finn'll start complaining.' He stooped to collect three small branches. 'There isn't much – you'd think there'd be a lot lying around,' he added, moving further in.

'Plenty of twigs,' Lisa remarked, collecting a handful and stowing them in the front pocket of her anorak.

'OK for starting a fire, but not much use for keeping it going,' came Matthew's voice from behind a thicket of holly. 'There's a bit more in here if you can squeeze through the prickles.'

'I've found a small dead log!' Lisa called back. 'And a decent pile of biggish twigs. It's odd there isn't more, though. We've seen no trace of any other hikers, and what else would collect firewood? Hardly the otters!'

'Dragons?' said Matthew with a grin, re-emerging, then wished he hadn't. Lisa had stopped and almost dropped her sizeable armful of large twigs.

'They *would* need firewood, wouldn't they?' she said softly, almost to herself. 'Oh, *please* let it be them!' He looked at her and was surprised to see her eyes full of tears. '*Please* let them still be alive and safe, and living in this lovely place!'

'Lisa …? ' he started, concerned, but she sniffed and seemed to come back to the present. 'I think that's enough for a fire tonight,' she said. 'If you can carry my log, I'll take those sticks.'

'I think I can manage both,' he tucked the log awkwardly under one arm, dropping a couple of sticks in the process. 'You walk behind and collect the droppings. Don't lose your twigs – we'll need the lot.' By unspoken consent, there was no more talk of dragons, not even as a joke. Matthew had not realised quite how seriously she was taking her search. He had hoped that the hiking and the wildlife would be enough, but now he was afraid that the failure of her self-imposed 'quest' would colour their whole expedition. He found himself grieving for her disappointment; it seemed inevitable.

By the time they got back to the camp, Finn had put the tents up, lit the Trangia and was starting to assemble pasta and sauce for a hot supper. They confessed the lack of a good wood supply, without mention of dragons – Lisa had herself well under control by the time they got back – but all agreed that it would be enough to keep them going for the first night, if they turned in early. Matthew suggested that dried rushes would make a good starting fuel, added to the scraps of paper wrapping they had carefully put aside, and went to collect a clump that he had spotted on the way. It took a fair number of matches but finally the little fire was well alight and the supper under way. Their smoke drifted over the loch as they sat close to the fire, the sky darkening and the silence deepening around them. The divers had reappeared at the far end of the loch and been identified – Black-throated – and Matthew happily got out his phone and added them to the list of birds he had started during the dig. They heard a faint sound of an animal coming down to drink across the water and the plop of fish rising.

'This place is glorious!' Lisa sighed happily, gazing up at the dark shapes of the surrounding mountains where a three-quarter moon was rising.

Matthew gazed up. 'Reminds me of bits of Wales. Snowdonia. Not far from home.'

'Can you speak Welsh?' Lisa asked curiously, realising that she'd never asked before.

'Not fluently. We moved there when I was twelve, so I didn't get taught in Welsh in Primary like all the rest. But enough to get by. My mates back home speak it all the time, so there's no choice really.'

'Awful age to move to a new school!' Finn commented. 'It's difficult to imagine when you've always lived in the same place, like us. And a different language! How on earth did you fit in?'

'My Dad's from Wales, and there were some distant relatives around, so it wasn't nearly as bad as I was afraid it would be. Everyone at school spoke English as well, so somebody always took pity on me and translated until I got the hang of it. You learn fast that way!'

'Being a student is a bit like living two separate lives, I think. Must be even more so for you. Not much chance of Welsh conversation in Edinburgh!' Lisa mused.

'It is a bit. And nobody calls me Matt back home – it doesn't fit the accent! Just don't ask me to say something in Welsh! That happens occasionally, when I meet new people, and it's really embarrassing.' Lisa, who had been about to say exactly that, was glad she hadn't.

'I think I'm ready for bed,' she said. 'I vote we leave the tents and stuff here tomorrow and go off exploring up the glen. We could try climbing Old Baldy if we're travelling light.'

'Could do,' Finn agreed. 'I can't see there's much risk, leaving our stuff here.'

'That's a plan then,' Lisa yawned. 'Night!'

The boys washed up at the edge of the loch, dowsed the last of the fire, and followed her.

On the far side of the water, the blue dragon, almost invisible in the gloaming, watched the lighted tents go dark, one by one. He got up, stretched his cramped wings, and crept slowly through the bracken towards the wood. When he was safely out of sight, he took off, flying low, and headed for Ollie's camp with his momentous news.

EMILY

Tom arrived just as the English family and Seamus were settling down for the night, but it was obvious as soon as he blurted out the news of the Human intruders that there was little chance of sleep that night. Alice immediately flew off up the mountain to fetch Emily and Des while Oliver stirred up the fire.

'Shall I go for Mum and Dad?' Tom was obviously itching for further action.

Oliver considered for a moment, but Ellen answered immediately. 'Yes, of course they must be told. We have to decide what's best to do, all together. I know Duncan worries more than the rest of us, but we can't keep this from him. Ollie, you go for them. Give Tom a breather.'

'I'm fine!' Tom protested, but Ollie was already on his way 'Don't leave Lily behind,' Georgie called after him, and Tom laughed. There was no chance of that!

While they waited, Seamus moved to sit beside Tom. 'Tell me about these Humans,' he said quietly. 'How many were there?'

'Just three. They put up those flimsy wee caves…' Seamus nodded. 'Tents,' he said. 'Where?'

'Right on the edge of the loch, on that sandy bit where the burn comes in. They came over the far ridge and then walked along by the loch-side. The otters saw them too. It was lucky I'd finished fishing and was drying my wings off behind our big rock, so I ducked down into the bracken and spied on them. I had to stay there for ages, but finally they went into their caves and it got dark enough for me to creep out and get back here without being seen.'

'Did they do anything else?'

'One stayed and built the caves up and the others went into the wood. They came out with firewood, and lit a fire and had a meal, and that's all really. I got pretty bored, just watching them. I thought Humans would be more interesting.'

'Believe me, they can be! Let's wait 'til everyone's here, then we can decide what we need to do. Well done, Tom!'

They both looked up as a flurry of wings heralded the arrival of Alice, with Des and Emily in a state of high excitement, and a few minutes later Ollie brought Duncan, Gwen and Lily to join them.

'Ollie's told us!' said Duncan, who was obviously very worried. 'We should leave as soon as possible. We can't risk ….'

'Hold on, Duncan,' Oliver said soothingly. 'Sit down and then we can decide what to do.'

'Better put the fire out!' Duncan wasn't listening. 'They'll see the smoke…'

'Dad, they're down by the big loch! Miles away!'

'And it's dark. Smoke might be a risk in daylight, but we have all night before there's any danger.' Ellen tried to keep the atmosphere calm.

'This has happened to us a good deal further south,' Oliver explained. 'Humans turn up too close for comfort, and we have to disappear. It's not difficult. They're not looking for us, remember. We don't exist!'

Gwen put a comforting talon on Duncan's arm, trying to calm his huffs. 'Listen to the others. They will know better what has to be done. Let's hear what Tom has to say first.'

Tom told his story again, adding a few extra details, and making the younger ones laugh as he demonstrated the pathetic attempts of Humans trying to light a fire. 'It's quite clever the way they can close their caves up, though,' he admitted.

'Tents!' chorused Emily and Alice, who constantly had to put the boys right on Human terminology. Gwen noticed Seamus smile and nod.

'What would *you* do, Seamus?' she asked. 'It seems to me that you have even more experience with Humans than Oliver, Ellen or Des. Give us your advice.'

Seamus frowned and thought for several seconds, while they waited expectantly. 'Tom, you said they spotted the otters?'

'Yes, they got all excited about them. And the divers. They stared at them through black things....'

'Binoccies,' said Emily promptly. 'Humans look at birds and things with them. I don't know why.'

'They didn't carry sticks and shoot fire at the divers? Or search for their nest? Or anything like that?'

'No. Good thing too – it's quite close to the rock. They might have spotted me!'

'Did they have any dogs with them?' Oliver put in.

'No.'

'Were they careful with their fire?'

'Seemed to be. They built it on the sand and stamped it out before going to bed, like we do.'

'These three Humans sound harmless,' Seamus declared to the group. 'But if you don't want to be seen we could either hide or move away altogether for a few days. There are enough of us to keep watch on them and warn of danger. If I am any judge, they won't be staying long.'

'What if they find our cave?' Duncan demanded. 'If they go in, they would realise that someone is living there.'

'That is the main risk, I agree, but if we're lucky they won't find it. Humans would find it difficult to scramble up Ben McIlwhinnie and they certainly couldn't climb the sheer face to the ledge of his knees. Your cave is invisible from below, behind his boots and the gorse bush, and you can cover your fireplace with earth. Even if they find and explore it, there is nothing in there that says, '*dragons live here*'! Obviously, none of us can hide *inside* the cave, just in case.'

'Why don't we hide in the back and attack them if they come in,' Ollie suggested eagerly. 'There are only three of them, and lots of us. We have fire! They'd never know what hit them!'

'No! That would bring Humans in their hordes,' Seamus warned. 'If Humans go missing, many *more* come to search for them. I have seen it happen at home. We need these three to think that there is nothing of interest in this glen – apart from the birds and otters they've already seen – and then they will go away. The ones with tents seldom stay anywhere for long. And Humans can't fly and spy from above; that's our big advantage.'

'Pity we can't wake Ben. He'd soon scare them off!' Lily remarked. She was thoroughly enjoying this crisis, Emily realised.

'That would be CERTAIN to bring the Humans!' Seamus exclaimed. 'A Mountain Giant! Even more of a myth than dragons. A pity, though. I would love to see him wake, and I envy you who have seen him walk,' he added, wistfully.

'Right – are we decided?' Des broke in briskly. 'Duncan, Gwen, Lily you leave the cave and come and hide out here with the rest of us. I think we should all stay together. But some of us can spread out and hide to keep watch on them tomorrow – see where they go and whether they pose any danger. Hopefully they'll move on, or go back to wherever they came from, but we mustn't lose sight of them until they do.'

'The most important thing to remember is that you mustn't fly unless it's essential,' Seamus warned. 'Stay under cover. If they see bracken moving, they'll assume it's some animal – they won't be thinking of dragons. In the air, you're much more likely to be spotted.'

'Duncan, you and Gwen go and make your cave look uninhabited, just in case they find it, then come back here. Lily and Georgie, you stay here. No argument! This is serious!' Oliver added as both opened their mouths to protest. 'Des, will you arrange the look-outs? And we'll need someone close to the camp to warn us in case they come this way and *we* have to hide. Humans won't force their way into bramble thickets luckily, so that shouldn't be difficult. We won't light a fire. We need to be in our places before dawn.'

'Be very wary of using Huff,' Ellen advised. 'It might make them suspicious. Let them think this is a boring, empty glen! If we see any of the local eagles or ospreys, we can ask them to keep clear too. They won't want Humans around either.'

Des and Seamus nodded, and went into a huddle with Tom and Ollie, Alice and Emily to allocate the look-out posts. Ellen touched Gwen's wing as she was preparing to leave with Duncan. 'Don't worry!' she whispered. 'I'm sure these Humans will go soon. I'll look after Lily.' Gwen nodded her thanks and followed a very worried Duncan back to the cave.

LISA

1

The plaintive cry of a curlew woke Matthew very early next morning. He rolled over onto his back, aware of a bruised hip, and checked the time. Just past six, and the sky was lightening. In fact, there was a pinkish glow through the thin canvas of his tent. There was no sign of movement from the others. As cautiously as he could, he crawled out of his sleeping bag, unzipped his tent and looked out at the morning. Amazing pink clouds covered half the sky. Sunrise. There was no wind, but the cold air stung his nose, and he hurriedly pulled on extra layers of clothes before venturing out, then stretched and tiptoed across the sandy ground to a convenient rock where he could sit more comfortably to put his boots on. Should he go across to collect wood before the others woke up? A bit of solitary exploration appealed, and the sound of a woodpecker drumming in the trees ahead decided him. He would walk the night's stiffness out of his legs, see if he could catch a glimpse of it and, hopefully, be back with firewood before the others emerged.

One of the otters surfaced close to the bank and watched him as he disappeared into the wood.

He followed the intermittent drumming on a slightly different path from the night before and was rewarded by the bright flash of the woodpecker in the trees ahead. 'Greater Spotted,' he noted silently, before turning his attention to the search for fallen wood. The ground beneath another of the wide-branched oaks, still thick with last-year's leaves proved more rewarding. With no idea that he was being watched from above, he filled his pockets with dry brown leaves and soon managed to collect as much wood as he could carry. His head was full of Lisa and the tears of the previous night as he set off back to the camp. He found himself wishing *he* could be the one to find dragons for her, and then laughed ruefully at himself. Good thing Finn wasn't here, reading his thoughts; he would probably challenge him to a duel! Or drive off with Lisa, abandoning him in the wilderness.... He came out of the trees and spotted one of the divers again. He was pretty sure he knew where their nest was, and his interest in the rare birds temporarily banished the thought of Lisa, dragons and Finn. When they got back from the day's hike, he would go and search for it, provided he could manage it without disturbing them.

As he approached the camp, Lisa's head emerged from the opening of her tent. 'How long have you been up?' she called, loud enough to cause a sudden movement and a groan from the third tent.

'Not long. There was a fantastic pink sunrise when I got up. I decided to get the wood, since I was awake.' He knelt and began to build a small fire, emptying his pockets of leaves. 'I hope this is enough to get it started,' he added doubtfully. 'Not sure I've got Finn's magic touch.'

'Add this,' Lisa handed him a crumpled chocolate wrapper. 'I've just eaten the last bit. Your dry reeds worked yesterday.'

'Good point. I'll get some. No point wasting matches.' As he got up, Finn emerged, scowling.

'Not much chance of a lie-in with you two about!' he complained. 'Lisa! Get some more clothes on, you'll catch your death!'

'OK, Mr Grumpy! Matt's been out to get your firewood, so don't start the day complaining! There's enough for a wee fire now, and a proper one later.' She disappeared inside her tent as Matthew came back with the reeds. To his secret satisfaction, he managed to get the fire going with a mere two matches, despite being aware of Finn's critical eye on the proceedings. 'Porridge OK for breakfast?' he called, finding three pots to heat up on the Trangia. 'Lovely!' said Lisa, emerging with a handful of sachets of demerara sugar to share around.

'You've been raiding a café!' Finn accused her.

'No – I just don't put it in my coffee! You don't *have* to have any, if you think it's stolen property.' Finn tutted in mock reproof, but he accepted three and sprinkled his porridge lavishly.

2

After breakfast, Lisa emptied her rucksack, which was the smallest, and they refilled it with food and drink for a day's hike. They plotted a route that led them through the wood to meet the burn that fed the loch at the top end and then, skirting the weird hill, they could head up the mountain, following the stream, and hope to reach the gorge by lunch-time. Lisa had insisted on exploring the gorge, and the boys knew – though they were careful not to mention it – that she reasoned it was the most likely place for caves.

It was difficult to hurry Matthew through the wood, as it was so full of birds. They all saw the woodpecker clearly, and heard another, and allowed him to stop and scan the trees once with his binoculars to determine the exact species of tits twittering high above. To Lisa's joy, he was able to spot a red squirrel peering at them from behind a trunk, and they all followed its leaping path from branch to branch in delight. Then they hustled him along and soon the trees thinned and they saw the strange hill in front of them. The burn ran alongside it to their right.

'Is it worth trying to climb it?' Finn wondered aloud. 'It's a weird outcrop! Must be some sort of glacial deposit. Those ledges look almost artificial, they're so regular.'

'It looks sheer in places,' Matthew said. 'Not sure it's worth it. The view will be even better further up. Pity though – that bald head is quite striking! I wonder what sort of rock it is.'

'Look, it's even got sticking-out ears!' Lisa said. 'It's a gorgeous hill! Wait while I take a photo. She moved into position and clicked her phone. 'Go and lean against one of those rocks at the bottom, you two,' she insisted. 'Gives an idea of its size. Got it. Thanks.'

'Right, up the burn towards the gorge?' said Finn, as she stowed her phone in her back pocket. 'There are faint tracks in the heather up there. Probably deer paths. There's been no sign of any proper paths since we left your dig site. It's obvious that nobody comes up here much.'

'That's what makes it perfect, even though it's slow going,' said Lisa happily as they forged a path through the heather. 'Oh look! Mountain hares!' They all turned to watch two hares, still bearing patches of winter white, race across the slope in front of them, leap the stream and disappear fast downhill. Alice, flat on the ledge of Ben McIlwhinnie's knees, took advantage of their distraction to crawl cautiously out of sight behind his fingers and send a single huff to Emily, concealed behind a rock higher up the hill near the entrance to the gorge.

'No sign of those eagles today,' Matthew remarked as they plodded upwards. 'Pity. They might nest in the gorge, though.'

'Not another stop!' warned Finn, forging ahead in the lead. 'You never warned me it was a bird-watching nut you were bringing,' he added over his shoulder to Lisa.

'Oh, come on, be fair!' Lisa panted, trying to keep up. 'You'd never have known what *sort* of woodpecker it was, without Matt.'

'I could carry the pack, if you like; make myself even more useful?' Matthew suggested.

'No way!' said Lisa. 'Then he'd be able to go even faster.' The slope became steeper and they decided to cut the banter and save their breath for the climb.

Emily, concealed behind her rock, watched the three tiny figures in the distance plodding slowly upwards and thought how wonderful it was to have wings.

There was a patch of scree before they crested the ridge and all three slipped and slithered as they tried to keep from falling. Even Finn was ready for a rest before tackling the gorge, so they sat in a row beside a copse of stunted rowan trees at the top, for a drink and some chocolate, facing the view down the glen. The far end of the loch, visible behind the trees, sparkled in the sunlight, and in the distance, they could just make out the old castle site. Away to their right they looked down on a larger area of woodland, and another glimmer of water. The dome of rock that they had christened 'Old Baldy' was the most noticeable feature in the landscape, the slope below it almost vertical on this side. 'It reminds me of something,' Lisa said, after they had gazed down for a few minutes. 'I'm sure I've seen something like it before, but I can't remember when. Ring any bells with you, Finn?' He shook his head and shrugged. 'Let's press on,' he suggested. 'I think I can hear a waterfall up ahead.'

Matthew took his turn with the rucksack, and they followed him up the hill. The ground became rocky and involved a good deal of scrambling with hands as well as feet. The sound of the waterfall grew louder, and soon they saw it, pouring down a sheer rock face and hurtling down the hill. 'There's a good deal of snow-melt in that,' Matthew said. 'It's probably just a trickle in summer.' They were coming nearer to patches of snow in sheltered gullies, and eventually the rocky walls of the gorge rose above them, with the stream winding between boulders at the foot. They picked their way carefully through the litter of rocks and smaller stones at the base of the sheer cliffs and made their way slowly up the gorge in single file, stopping from time to time to gaze up at the crags. Occasionally they were forced to cross the stream when it flowed against the rocks on their side. There were usually stepping stones, though often wobbly, and it was difficult to avoid putting a boot in the water.

Finally, they came to a wider part, where there was a tiny pebbly beach and a place that was reasonably dry to sit. The sun was overhead now, shining directly into the gorge, and it was a good deal warmer out of the wind.

'Food!' Finn demanded.

'Dry socks!' Lisa had just slipped into water deep enough to fill a boot.

'OK, OK!' said Matthew, swinging the rucksack off his back. 'Pack's all yours!' While they both scrabbled, Lisa in a side pocket and Finn in the main section, he trained his binoculars on the opposite wall. 'Nest up there,' he remarked. 'Ravens' I think. Yes, there's one on the crag.' As if it had heard him, the raven turned its head and seemed to gaze balefully at them. Then it spread huge black wings and took to the air. Its harsh croak sent echoes down the gorge, and they all flinched instinctively as it seemed to be heading straight at them. With another croak, it veered and headed up the gorge.

'Straight out of Hitchcock!' said Finn. 'I'd no idea ravens were that big.'

'It was definitely a warning!' Matthew agreed, still studying the crags. 'The mate's sitting on eggs. See that untidy heap of sticks? You can just see her head.' He passed the glasses to Lisa and accepted a roll and a handful of crisps.

Lisa, in possession of the binoculars, wasn't thinking about food. She had trained them a little further along the cliff. 'There's a cave!' she remarked, her casual tone fooling neither of her companions. 'See it? Along from the nest and down a bit. I wonder how deep it goes. Pity we can't explore it, but there's no way of getting up there, without rock-climbing gear.' She was moving the glasses along and down as she spoke. 'Looks as though someone's managed it, though. I can see the remnants of a fire on that ledge below it.'

'Probably those ravens practising nest-building,' said Finn indistinctly through a mouthful of roll, but Matthew followed her gaze. She passed his binoculars. 'See where I mean?'

'Yeah. And it does look a bit like a fireplace. If so, we're not the only people to have discovered this glen! I can't see any signs of rock-climbers, though – they usually leave pegs behind. I've never tried it, have you?' The others shook their heads.

Lisa picked up her neglected roll. 'Well, if there's one cave there might be more,' she said firmly, taking a bite.

'Honestly, you can laugh if you like, but this is the most dragonish place I've *ever* seen. Can't you imagine dragons living here? I can just see one, perched on that huge boulder in the middle of the stream, keeping watch for marauding humans!'

Concealed behind the rocks above their heads, Des started in surprise, and peered down at the boulder. Surely it couldn't be Emily…? She'd *promised* not to follow them…. No, nobody there. He swallowed a huff of relief, remembering Ellen's warning, relaxed and crouched down again, listening hard. He was beginning to be very curious about these three Humans.

'No dragon – but there is a dipper on the boulder,' Matthew pointed. 'See? Little dark brown bird with a white front. Gone, dived in. It'll probably come back.'

Finn had progressed to an apple and was unfolding the map. 'There isn't much more of the gorge,' he remarked. 'We can't see the end from here – it curves round, see? I think we're about halfway up. Shall we push on to the end? See if we can find a cave at ground level to keep Lisa happy.'

'And see if there's any sign of those eagles to keep *me* happy,' Matthew added. Above him, Des smirked. He knew *that* was unlikely! They had agreed to lie low.

'OK, I can eat my apple as we walk,' said Lisa, fighting to get her boot back on. 'Urrgh, this feels so cold and clammy!' she complained. 'My turn with the pack.' Both boys tried to take it for her, but she fixed them with an icy glare. Finn sighed.

'OK, Militant Feminist!' he said. 'Though we've eaten and drunk quite a lot of the weight, so it isn't *real* equality.' The punch that Lisa delivered nearly sent him floundering down the slope and into the stream.

Peace restored, they hiked on round the curve of the gorge, closely watched by the raven, which emitted another raucous croak before flying low over their heads and back to its crag. The dipper flew upstream ahead of them, low to the water, landing and bobbing amongst the rocks. The gorge narrowed and the ground rose, and finally, rounding the corner, they could see that it ended in a sheer wall of rock.

'No waterfall?' Lisa said, puzzled and rather disappointed. 'I thought there'd be a really dramatic one at the end.'

The reason was revealed when they reached the rock face; the stream emerged from the base, already in full flow.

'Wow!' said Finn. 'I've never seen that before! Reckon it's drinkable?'

'I don't see why not,' said Matthew. 'We could do with refilling the bottles. It'll be safer than the one beside the camp.' He squatted, scooped a handful and tasted it. 'Icy cold!' he said. Lisa joined him. 'That's *real* water,' she said. 'Lots better than tap! Pity the hole isn't high enough to crawl in. There might be proper caverns in there, with stalactites and things.'

Finn had been looking around. 'Bit of a cave up there, I think!' he called. 'Want to go in? Need I ask!' It was a little higher up the side of the gorge, but an easy scramble to the opening.

Lisa dumped the rucksack at the entrance and fished a small torch out of a side pocket. 'I brought this in case!' she said with satisfaction and shone the beam into the cave. It was not very deep, and they didn't really need the light, but it picked out shining veins of quartz and a trickle of water. At the end, the roof became a deep cleft running up into the hill, and to Lisa's joy, the torch beam found a small colony of roosting bats high up out of reach. They shuffled and peered in the torchlight but didn't fly down.

Cave explored to Lisa's satisfaction, they emerged into the sunlight, blinking. Then Matthew, staring up at the opposite wall, caught a flicker of movement at the top. He clutched Lisa's arm. 'Sssh – thought I saw something move up there. Don't move. Keep your eyes on the skyline.' The three of them froze. After a silent minute, Finn was just about to say that Matt must have been seeing things, when Lisa stiffened and pointed silently. A pair of slanted ears had appeared, framing a round striped face with big yellow eyes and a mouth that opened in an inaudible snarl. It stared down at them for a few seconds, then turned away. They caught a glimpse of a fat stripy tail as it vanished.

Matthew let out the breath he was holding. 'That was a Wildcat! I can't believe it!' He turned his gaze on Lisa, who was looking equally stunned. To his surprise she gave him an ecstatic hug.

'Good as a dragon?' he managed, feeling rather breathless.

'Nearly!'

'Yeah, pretty good!' Finn admitted. 'But I think we'd better be heading back. It's just after three, and we don't want to be caught in the dark.' He carefully filled the three water bottles at the stream, without looking at the others, and then shouldered the rucksack. This time Lisa didn't argue.

They moved faster on the way down, as Finn set a good pace, leaving little time to look around. Their progress down the scree was dangerously fast, but they managed to reach smoother ground with ankles intact. Matthew still scanned the skies for eagles whenever he could but was too elated by the wildcat to be disappointed when they failed to appear.

When they finally reached the edge of the wood, they stopped for a breather. 'If we take a different route through here, we can collect more wood for tonight,' Lisa suggested. 'Or we could go further over that way and check out that bigger patch of woodland we saw from the top. It's not that late. We were much faster coming down, 'specially on the scree.'

'It's further than it looks,' said Matthew, who wanted to get back to the camp in time to search for the divers' nest before dark.

'We could explore that way tomorrow, then,' Lisa persisted. 'It looked as though there was another loch in the middle. There might be ospreys there – we haven't seen any yet. Weren't they on your wish list, Matt?'

Finn stared at her. 'We need to start back tomorrow,' he said.

'No!' Lisa exclaimed. 'We've only just got here! There's loads more to see!'

'Work it out,' said Finn. 'We left on Monday. We said we'd be away five days. It's end of Wednesday now.'

'Is it? I've lost count,' said Lisa vaguely.

'It'll take a full day's walking even to get to that hostel site. Then we've got to hike back to the car before we can start the drive home. Steve's coming to pick it up at the weekend – he wasn't sure exactly when, but it more than my life's worth not to be there to hand it over. Sorry, no choice!'

Matthew looked from one to the other. He felt Lisa's disappointment keenly and shared it. But without Finn and his borrowed car, they would never have been able to come at all. There was no help for it; they would have to go.

'You're right, Finn,' he said. 'I'd lost track of the days too. Sorry Lisa! We can't risk being late, and it's easy to get delayed. Any one of us could turn an ankle and slow us down. We'll have to pack up tomorrow. Let's get back and make the most of the last evening. Think how much we've seen in just two days!'

Lisa nodded without speaking, picked up the backpack and headed round the edge of the wood, searching for another route through. The boys followed without looking at each other; Finn frowning and obviously determined, Matthew pondering why.

EMILY

1

As the three Humans slithered and tramped their way down the hill, passing Ben with barely a second glance, Des cautiously descended the gorge and crept through the bracken to Emily's hiding place. 'They're heading back to the wood,' he said. 'They haven't looked back once. I think it's safe to go down to Alice. If we creep over that rise, we can fly low. I spotted Tom from the top while they were safely in the gorge. He's back in the lookout tree. He must have left it to report to Ollie back near the camp as soon as they reached the gorge. He'll let us know when they're safely back by the loch.'

Alice was delighted to see them. 'I was afraid they'd come up and find the cave,' she said, 'but they just had a good look at Ben from down there and only got as far as his boot. I heard one say *it's a gorgeous hill*! If only they knew!'

Emily chuckled, 'I felt so sorry for them, tramping up to the gorge – especially when they kept slithering on the stony bit.'

'And I overheard a rather interesting conversation!' Des added. 'No, I'm not telling you now. Wait 'til we're all together. Where are they now?'

'Disappeared into the wood. Are we safe to head for the camp?'

'Better wait 'til they're further in, but we should be safe to go down to the cave.' Des dropped behind the gorse bush and headed inside. Alice and Emily followed and found him rummaging among Gwen's stores, hidden at the far end. He came out with a talon-full of dried toad-stools and passed them round. 'I hope the others have managed to get some supper going,' he remarked. 'It's been a long day. I'm starving!'

'Keep an eye on the tree,' Emily said. 'Tom should signal when it's safe to head down.'

It was not long before a single huff from Tom told them that the Humans were almost through the wood and one by one, flying low, Emily, Alice and Des flew round the back of Ben, skirted the trees and headed towards the camp.

The parents were waiting for news and were very relieved to hear that the cave was safely undiscovered. They had spent much of the day fishing, and a fine catch of loch trout was laid out waiting until it was considered safe to light a fire. 'Brilliant!' said Des. 'How did you get round the ospreys?' A pair nested every year in a tree at the far end of the loch and considered they had special fishing rights. The dragons understood this, and they had all come to a wary understanding over the years.

'We told them it was an emergency,' Ellen said. 'Fortunately, they feel much the same about Humans.'

'It's not as if there's a shortage of fish,' Oliver added. 'The loch's teeming with them! Reckon we could get a fire going now?'

'Let's wait 'til Tom reports back, just in case. Think I'll go for a quick swim.'

'Lily and Georgie are down there.'

'Thanks for the warning!' Des headed down to the loch as Ollie flew in from his look-out point.

'That went pretty well!' he said with satisfaction. 'They haven't a clue, have they? I'm for a swim too.'

Emily and Alice settled down to talk over their day together. 'Honestly, there was no problem at all!' Emily claimed. 'I don't think this sort of Human is dangerous, even if they have those binoccy things. Not like the ones we know about on the high moors, who kill the grouse with fire-sticks.'

'Talking of grouse, Seamus went to get some once you were safely in position and on guard,' Gwen said, overhearing them. 'He headed the other way, to be safe. He should be back soon. He really is a great help with his hunting. I'll miss him when he goes back to Ireland!' Alice and Emily exchanged a wary glance. They didn't think the four parents were aware that Tom and Ollie, and possibly the rest of their offspring too, were planning on travelling back with him.

Fortunately, Tom landed in their midst at that point, dripping wet and bursting with news. 'I had a quick dip on the way back,' he panted. 'The others are coming. It's safe to get the fire going.' He shook himself violently, showering Alice and Emily with water. 'They're bringing some extra fish. Even Lily caught one! We've lots to tell you!'

A few minutes later the fire was lit, the fish were speared and cooking (with Des in charge making sure they were well blackened) and the dragons gathered round, eager to share the day's news. Seamus, carrying a fine haul of grouse, arrived just in time and joined the circle round the fire. One by one, the young dragons told how the three Humans had packed a bag, left the camp with their 'caves' closed up, walked through the wood, stopped to admire the *'gorgeous hill'* – which caused laughter all around the circle – missed the cave and climbed to the gorge, obviously unaware that a number of dragons were spying on their every move. Des was the last to give his report.

'They spotted our cave, Em!' he said, turning the fish over carefully. 'They were sitting opposite it looking through those binoccies at the ravens' nest. The old bird saw and flew right at them! I couldn't see whether he actually *hit*, but probably not. I'd have heard the screams. I heard them mention the cave, but obviously they couldn't get up the cliff, so there wasn't any real danger. Then they walked right along to where the stream comes out and poked about a bit, before starting back. It takes them ages to get anywhere, poor things!' Emily waited for him to mention the 'interesting conversation', but she caught a warning glint in his eye and decided to say nothing.

'I listened-in to them talking too,' Tom said, happily aware that he was bringing the most important piece of news. 'And they're leaving tomorrow! Back the way they came. They argued a bit and then decided. So, we can stop worrying, Dad! I'll go down early and make sure they've really gone.' The news was greeted with huffs of relief and the dragons settled down happily to devour their scorched fish. Only Emily felt a surge of disappointment. Across the fire, she saw Seamus watching her and wondered if he shared it. And when would she learn about that *conversation*?

'Are you going back to your cave tonight, Mum?' she asked as they finished the meal with hot nettle tea, passing mugs around to share it.

'Better wait until we're sure they've left,' Duncan answered for her. 'We'll stay here until tomorrow.' 'Yess!' said Lily, pleased. Gwen sighed but agreed to keep the peace, though she would obviously have preferred to go home. Des looked across at Emily.

'We'll get back up to ours, shall we? They're hardly going to trek back up there again in the dark! Fancy coming too, Seamus?' he added casually. Seamus smiled and nodded, getting up to follow them. As they left, Ollie and Tom were giving their audience an exaggeratedly funny imitation of Humans climbing a hill, and Lily could be heard loudly demanding that she and Georgie be allowed to go with Tom to watch them leaving in the morning. 'Any bets on who'll win that one?' Des asked as they left the firelight behind.

2

Back at the cave, the three of them settled inside, without risking a more visible fire, and Des passed round some of his precious Firewater. 'Right,' said Emily firmly, 'tell us about this conversation you overheard. I'm dying to know! I thought you were going to tell everyone.'

'I changed my mind. But I want Seamus to hear. I was hidden up there, right above where they were sitting having a rest, when one of them said – the female it was – *it's the most dragonish place I've ever seen. I can imagine dragons living here.* Then I nearly jumped out of my scales when she added *I can see a dragon on that rock keeping watch.* I thought she might have seen you, Em! It gave me a real shock! But when I calmed down and looked, I realised there was no one there. Don't know what on earth she was talking about. Wasn't that weird? What do you think, Seamus?'

'I've no idea what she meant,' Seamus replied, thoughtfully, 'but Humans do know about dragons – or think they do. Perhaps she was talking about a book she'd read. We come into lots of their books.' Emily nodded; she and Alice had discovered that. 'But the more I hear about these three, the more I think they *are* the right sort of Human. Emily, if you *really* want to do as your Gran suggested and try to make friends, this seems to me the best opportunity you will ever have.'

'You think we should show ourselves to them?' Des asked, after a thoughtful pause. Emily listened, and held her breath, willing him to agree.

'Yes, I do. A single Human would be better – who would believe her? But three is not too big a risk. These three seem to love the wild, or why would they visit this glen and sleep on the ground and cook on a fire like dragons? A pity they're leaving tomorrow, but if we visit them early it might be time enough.'

'Just us three?' Des asked. Emily let out her breath. It sounded as though he was going to agree.

'Yes! One alone might be in danger, more would seem threatening. The last thing we must do is let them flee before we have spoken to them and shown ourselves friendly. No breathing fire!'

'No Tom and Ollie then!'

'I wish we could take Alice with us, though,' said Emily. 'I hate leaving her out.'

'Have we agreed to do it?' Des asked.

Emily glared at him. 'Of course we have! Seamus is absolutely right. It's the best chance we could possibly have, and we mustn't lose a minute. They're not likely to leave in the dark, are they?' she appealed to Seamus, who was listening and watching her with amused appreciation. 'Tomorrow then, just before dawn and just us three. Oh, thank you, Seamus! That advice was just what we needed. I'm so glad you came to find us!'

Seamus inclined his head politely and rose. 'And so am I! Time for sleep, if we are to be down at the loch before dawn.' The others got up as well. Emily indicated the pile of heather near the door, beamed at him and then gave him a quick hug before turning to hug Des as well. 'Thank you!' she breathed into his ear and allowed herself to be shepherded to the back of the cave.

'Desmond, you are a most fortunate dragon!' Seamus murmured as he settled down to sleep.

REUNION

1

Although Finn had won the argument, he did not relax over fire-lighting and cooking and Lisa was obviously still bitterly disappointed. It was rather a strained supper. Afterwards, in the dusk, Matthew left the other two alone while he crept as quietly as he could round the opposite shore of the loch, where he thought the divers might have their nest. He hid behind a rock and spotted them sitting together but was unable to see whether there were eggs in the nest. He did have a good view of both otters from this side of the loch and was sure the hole just visible on the bank was a holt. They seemed to be sharing the remains of a fish on a large boulder, undisturbed by the presence of three people camping close by. He wished Lisa had been there to see them too.

When he got back to the tents, he discovered that she had gone to bed, and Finn was finishing a mug of coffee, staring moodily across the water. 'Think I'll turn in too,' he said. 'Better make an early start tomorrow, I suppose. We've been dead lucky with the weather. This place would be a bit bleak in pouring rain.'

'Don't tempt fate – we've still got a day to go,' was the unpromising response. He gave up and crawled into his tent. Finn stamped out the last remnants of the fire with unnecessary force and did the same.

Even though Matthew spent a restless night, troubled by the loss of the easy-going friendship of the trip so far, he still woke at dawn. He knew it was no good trying to get back to sleep, and, as usual, he was stiff after a night on the ground. He would get up without waking the others; perhaps pay a final early-morning visit to the woodland birds.

When he was dressed, he unzipped the tent, put his head out and stifled a cry of astonishment and alarm.

Standing upright on the large boulder that dominated the opposite bank was a dragon. She was standing perfectly still, outstretched wings glowing pink in the rosy dawn light, and was staring straight at him down her long nose. The sight was so amazing that, at first, he didn't register the other two, flanking her on the ground at the base of the rock, and equally still and silent and staring. For a couple of minutes, which felt a lot longer, he froze. If he moved, would they attack? Fly away? He had to risk it; Lisa *must* see them. Moving very slowly, never taking his eyes off the motionless dragons, he eeled his way across to her tent and whispered her name urgently. Three pairs of eyes followed his movement, but to Matthew they seemed as still as statues. Still not daring to take his eyes off them, he said, 'Lisa!' a little more loudly, and heard her stir inside the tent. 'Lisa, it's me, come out, very slowly…. quietly…. You *have* to see this….' The tent shook as she wriggled out of her sleeping bag and he heard the zipper slide.

'What is it?' she started to whisper, then 'Oh! Oh Matt! It's Emily – I know it is. Wake Finn.' She stood up slowly, while Matthew crawled behind her tent to Finn's and spoke his name more loudly. If the miraculous dragons took fright and flew away, at least she had seen them. As Finn's voice mumbled, 'What the….?' he said urgently, 'Come'n see this! Quick!'

Still in his sleeping bag, Finn poked his head out of his tent. As he saw the dragons, his expression changed. 'My God!' he whispered.

Lisa had advanced to the water's edge. The boys could see her shivering as they both stood up cautiously and moved to stand behind her. Without looking round, she called 'Emily! Emily! It's me, it's Lisa! You remember me, I *know* you do. Fly over here! Please!'

It was as if three statues had come alive. Emily let out a huff of astonishment, glanced at the other two, and took off across the loch, landing in a flurry on the sand. Des followed close, hovered above her, and landed in the shallows, scattering spray. He looked even bigger than Finn remembered, and he was not at all sure of their safety. Lisa had no such concern.

'Oh Emily, you're so much bigger! You do remember me, don't you? And Finn? And this is Matt – you don't know him, but he's a friend – you can trust him.'

Emily glanced briefly at the boys, then looked Lisa up and down, drew a deep breath and let out a slow thoughtful huff. 'Lisa, you look so different! And I wouldn't have known it was Finn! Are you what they call *grown-ups* now?'

'Not really! But *you* are, I can see! And Des....' She looked at him, uncertainly. Des had always been more suspicious of them in the past. 'Does Des mind me talking to you?'

Emily glanced behind her and sighed. 'Oh Des! Stop *looming*! Go and tell Seamus it's all right. These are the very best kind of Human – they're *friends.* He thinks he has to protect me,' she added to Lisa, who chuckled. 'I know the feeling!' she said, indicating her own bodyguard.

Des sent a huff across the loch and beckoned Seamus with a flick of his head. He flew across the water, bronze and gold glinting in the rising sun and bowed politely to the little group. 'I have spoken with Human friends before, at home in Ireland,' he said, formally. 'I am glad to meet you, and we mean you no harm.'

Emily glared pointedly at Des, who allowed himself to relax a little. 'All right, that goes for me too!' he said. 'It's years since we last saw you, and nobody has ever come looking for us. You must have kept our secret. But what are you doing here? Humans *never* come this far up the glen.'

'Matt and I came with an archaeology group two weeks ago,' Lisa told him. We were digging at the old castle site, down there. I don't suppose you realised....' She stopped. Des and Emily had looked at each other, and both were grinning broadly.

'Oh, we knew all right!' Des said. 'We kept watch on you for three weeks. It got pretty boring, just watching you scrape around in those squares.'

'Was it you who looked up the Glen with those binoc-cy things?' Emily asked Matthew.

'Yes, I'm sorry. I didn't mean any harm. I saw some smoke near that weird-shaped hill and wondered what it was,' said Matthew, speaking for the first time. Des and Emily exchanged a glance and she understood. There must be no mention of Ben McIlwhinnie!

'And you were curious, of course,' Seamus said. 'But you are all cold, I think. I'll light a fire for you.' He took off in the direction of the wood and returned very quickly with a sizeable load. Within seconds a fire was blazing cheerfully. Finn let out an admiring whistle and Seamus laughed. 'It is a thing we are good at!' he said.

'We need to get dressed!' Lisa realised. 'You won't disappear, will you?' she added over her shoulder and dived into her tent. Finn followed but Matthew, already dressed, looked from Des to Emily, hesitated, then made up his mind, hoping they would not be angry or upset.

'I saw you too, years ago. It was in Wales, by the sea. You were with three others, and there was a raft, alight and floating out to sea.'

'You were in that round-red flying-thing!' Emily gasped. 'It flew with dragons' breath. You waved to us. There were two others. We were saying farewell to my Gran, on the beach.'

Matthew nodded. 'We thought it was something like that. And later, on the clifftop, we spotted you again, before you flew away. I don't think you saw us that time.'

'Three of you,' Des's voice had hardened. 'And the others – did they keep our secret too?'

'Yes. I - I know they did.' Matthew tried hard to keep his voice steady as he looked directly at Des, who nodded slowly. Lisa came back, wearing several more layers, and handed Matthew his anorak. 'Thanks,' he said. 'I've told them,' he added in an undertone as he pulled it on.

'Good.' She gave him a delighted grin. 'Let's sit down. What a gorgeous fire! Emily, tell me – is Tom here as well? Where do you live? Do you have a cave somewhere? We hiked up the mountain to that gorge yesterday, and spotted one high up on the cliff, but we couldn't get to it….' She stopped, realising that all three dragons were smiling broadly. 'Don't tell me! You know about that as well?'

'We had you tracked all the way!' said Des. 'I was above you when you stopped in the gorge. I listened to you talking and was puzzled when you mentioned dragons. Now I understand. Emily and I live in the cave you spotted.'

'You and Emily!' Lisa said, delighted.

'The rest of my family live in a cave further down the mountain,' Emily continued. 'But Tom spends a lot of time travelling with Ollie – remember him?'

'I certainly do!' said Finn. 'He was never keen on us. He's not around is he?'

'Yes, and Alice too.'

'Oh, I'd love to see Alice again! Ollie was a lot friendlier when Megan and I found that gorgeous bolshie baby, Finn. I'm sure he'll be OK. Oh, what about the baby?'

'No longer a baby!' Des said ruefully, 'but just as bolshie. She's here too.'

'Sounds like a whole *herd* of dragons…' said Finn, tactlessly.

'You mean *Family!* Or even better, *Clan!*' Lisa glared at him, horrified.

'How on earth do you stay hidden with so many of you?' Finn ignored her.

'By being clever and cunning,' said Des rather coldly, ignoring the warning nudge of Emily's tail.

'I think it's time for you to meet the Clan,' Seamus interjected, before the tone could cool further. 'Can we lead them to the cave? It's nearer than the forest camp, and we can share a meal and talk. We have a good store of grouse. You can eat roast grouse? I have eaten with Humans before, so I promise not to let Des blacken yours, even though that's the way *we* like it. You can meet Duncan and Gwen, Emily's parents, and Ellen and Oliver, the English dragons.

'Then there's the youngsters, Georgie and Lily, of course.' Des added.

The three students looked at each other, hesitating.

'You will be quite safe, even though there are so many of us,' Seamus assured them.

'It's not that. We need to leave today. In fact, we should be packing up right now,' Finn said.

Lisa turned to him passionately. 'Finn! We can't go *now*! We'll never, never get a chance like this again. There must be a way to stay for today, at least. Please! *Please*!' She was almost in tears. Emily put a comforting talon on her arm, then took her hand. Finn shook his head, stubbornly.

'Sorry, we have to get back. We can't!' he said.

'There might be a way,' said Matthew tentatively, and Lisa turned to him in desperation. 'Matt! Please think of one!'

'How?' said Finn. The dragons waited quietly; Emily was still holding Lisa's hand.

'It's early still. If we pack up the tents now, we could go up to the cave this morning, meet all your dragon friends, share their grouse, and then come back to pick our stuff up this afternoon. There should be time to hike to the dig site to camp tonight, which would mean we could get all the way to the car from there tomorrow, before it gets dark. We could easily drive back to Glasgow overnight, and be back in time to hand the car over. We can share the driving. Please, Finn! I agree with Lisa – we can't miss this chance. It's amazing – unique! Worth missing a night's sleep!'

There was a long silence, then Finn said, 'I suppose that might work. I want to see Ollie and the rest too,' he admitted. Lisa heaved a deep sigh and beamed at him in relief.

'Then we are all agreed,' said Seamus as Des nodded too. 'I'll fly to the camp to warn the others.' He spread his wings and soared across the loch.

'Pity you're too big to carry up the hill,' Des remarked. 'I used to give *you* rides when you were wee, didn't I, Wattie?' He turned and addressed the otter, who had crept out of the water behind them without being noticed and was listening to their talk. The boys and Lisa whirled round, amazed. The otter barked back at him. 'I don't believe this!' said Matthew. 'Don't tell me *they* can talk as well?' The otter stared at him, gave another bark, which sounded remarkably like *'Naaa!'*, dived into the loch and vanished.

'Put some water on to boil, Matt,' Finn said. 'I need tea while we're packing up. He disappeared into his tent. Matthew, turning to his own tent, stopped. 'Stay and talk to Emily,' he said to Lisa. 'I'll help with yours when I've done mine.' Lisa smiled her thanks.

'Good,' said Emily. 'Why don't you fly up and help Seamus?' she said to Des. 'I know how much you hate walking!'

'Will you be all right?'

Emily rolled her eyes. 'You're doing it again!' she said. 'Looming! Hovering! Why shouldn't I be all right? Go away! I want to talk to Lisa.'

'All right, I'm going! I know when I'm not wanted!' He spread his wings, and Emily blew him a fond huff as he took off. 'He can't help it!' she said.

'He's not nearly as frightening as he used to be,' said Lisa. 'I think it's lovely that you and he are - are sharing a cave now. Do you live there all the time?'

'We go travelling a lot. He was always the expert Traveller, remember? Well, I loved it when he took me to Wales to say goodbye to Gran – the time your friend saw us. So now we travel and explore together. There's so much wild country further north, and we fly over the sea too. I love it, though it's always nice to get back to our Glen.'

'You don't have any wee dragons, then?'

'Not yet. Des keeps hinting, but *I* think there's plenty of time. We would have to stay at home!'

'What about Alice? Has she found someone too?'

Emily looked sad. 'No. There are so few dragons, you see. We're planning to travel to Ireland with Seamus soon, so maybe… And you – you have *two* boys! Or men? Do I call them *men* now? I remember that Finn was your friend, but who is this other one who spotted us near the Gramps' cave in Wales?'

Lisa, glad that both her companions were too busy with tents to overhear this conversation, was starting to explain about University and her new life as a student when Alice appeared, flying low and fast, and landed beside them. 'Des came to tell me,' she explained, beaming at Lisa. 'I couldn't wait to see you! I still have your gift – look!' She held out a talon to show the battered blue hair bobble, worn round her wrist, which Lisa had given her so long ago.

'Mine fell off and got lost,' Emily admitted. 'But I use Gran's gift to remind me of you.'

'Isn't Megan with you?' Alice asked, looking around.

'She's still at school, so has shorter holidays. She remembers you though. I wish we could have brought her!'

The water in the pan boiled and Matthew came over to make tea. Lisa introduced Alice, who glanced from him to Finn and smiled knowingly. Lisa reflected that these female dragons seemed to understand Humans better than they did themselves!

'I've just flown North with my family,' Alice said. 'I love this Glen. I'm so pleased we'll be here for another summer.'

'You're right, it's beautiful,' said Matthew. 'And the wildlife is amazing! We even caught a glimpse of a wild-cat yesterday, up above your gorge. They're incredibly rare.' He sounded diffident, obviously still uncomfortably aware that he was talking to creatures from his fantasy fiction, and wondering if he was dreaming, Lisa thought, amused.

'That'd be Archie,' Emily said. 'He was born in our cave a few years ago. The rest of the family disappeared, but he still comes back from time to time. Tom sort-of adopted him.' Matthew shook his head, feeling even more unreal, and took a mug of tea to Finn, who was dismantling Lisa's tent. A few minutes later, Finn called Lisa over to pack her own bag and came himself to greet Alice. He seemed to have accepted that they were going to be a bit later arriving back in Glasgow and was obviously looking forward to seeing Ollie again.

'I suppose it'll be OK leaving the stuff here while we go up the hill,' he said to the others as they strapped up the packs and finished their coffee and a make-shift breakfast of cereal bars. Lisa offered one to Emily and Alice, carefully removing the wrappers first, and was delighted to find that they liked them. Rummaging in the depths of her pack, she discovered that she had quite a number left and decided to fill her pockets in case they could be shared in return for the promised grouse.

'Don't forget tomorrow's trek. We finished the gingerbread,' Finn warned. The others had to agree that supplies were getting low, but Matthew whispered, 'I've got some left,' as he buckled his rucksack, and she thought she saw him pocket another four as they set off, escorted by Alice and Emily.

2

The walk round the loch and through the woods in the early morning, unhurried, unencumbered by backpacks and accompanied by the two bright dragons, was a magical experience for all three of them. The otter resurfaced, bringing his mate, and lolloped along the bank ahead of them, before diving back, rolling and tumbling in the water. 'They have two tiny cubs in the holt over there,' said Emily, 'but they're too small to bring out to show you. They've been keeping watch on you since you arrived but had already decided you were harmless.'

'Can we come back in a few weeks to see them?' Lisa asked Finn, only half joking.

'Are the divers always here?' Matthew asked, spotting one fishing at the far end of the loch.

'They arrived just this spring,' Emily answered. 'They're still a bit wary of us. Some birds are, you know. The ospreys think we steal their fish. And our local ravens are quite hostile.'

'We noticed!' said Finn. 'It tried to attack us in the gorge yesterday.'

'Are there ospreys round here?' Matthew asked eagerly. 'I've never seen one.'

'Yes, there's a pair on our loch over there,' said Alice, waving a wing. 'They nest there every year.' Matthew sighed in disappointment, realising that it would be a trek too far on this trip.

Emily was able to point out two red squirrel drays high in the old oaks, and the woodpecker's drumming led them easily to its nest hole. The constant twitter of small birds gave Matthew a cricked neck as he walked with his eyes up, frequently tripping over roots and stones as he tried to identify them. Several squirrels made an appearance, apparently unafraid of dragons. 'It's good, being an honorary dragon,' Lisa remarked. 'You see so much more!'

Their path through the wood had meandered, but eventually they came to the edge and saw the distinctive shape of Lisa's 'gorgeous hill' ahead and to the left. Unlike the apparently deserted place of the previous day, it was alive with activity. Two dragons, gold and orange, were perched on the smooth summit; a fire was burning on the lowest ledge, where Des sat, apparently surrounded by a moving whirl of brown; other coloured shapes moved purposefully around, disappearing behind the huge gorse bush from time to time. Then there was a wild flurry of wings, and Tom and Ollie wheeled round the far side of the hill and headed straight for them. Finn and Matthew flinched involuntarily, but Lisa waved wildly in delight as they swooped over their heads and came to earth just in front of them. 'Finn!' said Ollie, holding up a wing for a High Four. 'Good to see you!' Finn, with a delighted grin, stepped forward and raised a hand. Ollie was bigger than he remembered and Tom, though the smaller of the two, seemed enormous when he recalled the small blue dragon of their earlier meeting.

'Where's Charlie?' Tom enquired, looking hard at Matthew and realising that this wasn't his footballing friend.

'Not with us,' said Lisa. 'This is Matt. Charlie's so mad on football these days that I think he's forgotten he ever met a dragon.'

As Tom beamed and opened his mouth to speak again, Emily said hurriedly, 'Don't get him started on Tail-Stane! Come and meet the others. I warn you, Dad's very wary when it comes to Humans, so don't worry if he seems a bit hostile. Mum'll be fine.'

They plodded up the slope towards the gorse bush. Des, plucking grouse with the efficiency of long practice, waved a wing and grinned with Emily as he saw Matthew looking curiously at the two identical brown rocks on either side of the gorse bush and the fire place. Duncan, carrying firewood, emerged from the hidden cave and stopped dead when he saw them. The huff with its hint of flame was *definitely* hostile, but Tom rushed on with the introductions, and the tension was eased when Gwen, following him out, gave the three students a much friendlier greeting. Lisa liked her immediately.

'Can we show them the cave?' Emily asked her mother. 'Obviously they can't fly up to ours, but they'd like to see inside this one, wouldn't you?' She turned to Lisa, who was looking puzzled.

'Cave? Where?' she asked, but Finn had guessed. 'Behind the bush?' he asked, and Emily nodded and led the three of them round to show them the low cave entrance.

'It's brilliantly well hidden! We never guessed it was here when we passed yesterday,' said Matthew admiringly as Emily led the way in, sending up a huff of flame to light the inner chambers.

'This used to be my room,' Emily said. 'It's Lily's now. Those are her drawings on that flat bit of wall. I used to write stories on it, but there was never enough room. Tom's is next door, when he isn't off with Ollie, and this little one is used for stores of wood and things. We found old bones in it when we first moved in, so we always call it the Bone Cave. Mum and Dad's is round the corner, over there.'

'It's a fantastic cave,' said Lisa. 'People would love to explore this, so it's a good thing it's so well hidden.'

'I wonder what creature left its bones.' Matthew's interest in archaeology came to the fore. 'Could I go in and see? I've brought a torch.' Emily nodded, and he disappeared behind the stacked wood, treading carefully. Finn, less interested in bones, went out to talk to Ollie and Tom while Lisa surveyed the stores on the rock shelves, fascinated by weird dragon delicacies. But before she could learn much about them, there was a flash of gold and Lily bounced in, and flung her wings round her.

'I was that wee dragon you rescued!' she declared. 'Do you remember? I was up a tree. Those creatures of yours were shouting at me. Isn't Megan here? I really liked

Megan! She wanted me to stay with her! She wrapped me up in her coat. Did you think I'd be as big as this? You're bigger, but you haven't grown as much as me! Are you going to stay?' It was obvious that the stream of questions could carry on indefinitely, but at that moment, Duncan came in for more wood, and frowned.

'Lily, that's enough!' he said firmly.

Emily stopped him as he headed towards the Bone Cave. 'Matt's in there. He was interested in the bones. I said he could, so don't get all huffy and frighten him to death! You might set the wood on fire.' Her father scowled at her but said nothing. Emily sighed. 'He's not always like this,' she said to Lisa. 'It's just that all his life he's avoided Humans.'

'It's all right. We understand. But I hope he knows that *we're* no danger to you. Really, we're not!'

'The rest of us know that. We'll work on him!' They went out into the sunshine, where Lily introduced Georgie, who seemed too shy to speak. 'I wish we could take you up to Ben's head,' she said, oblivious to the look of horror that passed between Emily and Des, 'but you need to be able to fly. You'd never manage to climb up on feet. It's our favourite place to keep watch. Not that we need to keep watch really. Nothing dangerous or exciting ever happens here. Apart from those diggers, down by the castle, and you of course.'

As she paused for breath, Lisa said, '*Ben's Head!* That's a lovely name for the top of the hill! Like Ben Nevis and Ben Lomond and all the other Bens. We thought it looked like a bald head when we saw it in the distance, didn't we, Matt?' A shaken-looking Matthew had just emerged from the cave, dusting his hands together. As Lisa turned to look at him, Des was able to hiss 'Ssshh!' at Lily while her back was turned. Lily, remembering the rule that the Mountain Giant was not to be mentioned, sang out 'Sorry!' and mercifully stopped talking. Emily heaved a sigh of relief.

'What is it?' Lisa asked Matthew quietly while the dragons seemed preoccupied.

'Those bones – they're *ancient*, and some of them are enormous! I'd love to know what creature they belonged to. I wish I could take one back for analysis.'

'Don't even *think* of it!' Lisa whispered, and he nodded, ruefully. 'Suppose not!' They turned to watch as Gwen swept the grouse feathers into a pile with her tail, then scooped a talonful and carried it into the cave. 'They're nice and soft on beds!' she explained. Emily collected a double handful and followed her.

'Did you say you wanted to see the eagles?' Des broke in from his place by the fire, where he was threading plucked grouse onto sticks. 'Here they come!' Two majestic golden eagles spiralled down, circling Ben's Head and then swooping low with screaming cries over the assembly by the fire. They yelped greetings at Des and the dragons, tilted their heads to eye the humans with suspicion, and then headed for the far woods. 'Wow!' said Lisa in delight, rushing out of the cave, and even Finn looked up, impressed. Matthew gazed after them, mesmerised, as they disappeared.

'I didn't think we'd see them again. There was no sign of them yesterday,' he remarked.

'Ah, yes!' said Des. 'That might have been our fault. Sorry. It was before we knew who you were. We decided this Glen had to seem very boring for invading Humans, so warned them to stay away. We told the ospreys too just in case you wandered over that way.'

'It's certainly not boring! We even caught a glimpse of a wildcat at the top of the gorge,' said Matthew.

'No point trying to give orders to a cat,' said Duncan. 'Especially not that one!'

'He'll probably be along later, if he's around,' said Tom. 'He's called Archie,' he added, for the benefit of the visitors. 'He was born here in the cave a few years ago. We haven't seen his mother or sisters for ages, but he often turns up.'

'Especially when there's food on offer,' Ollie added. He and Tom were sitting, with Finn between them, on the strange brown rock that, unknown to the visitors, was actually Ben's right boot. Lily pulled Lisa back into the cave to show off her wall pictures, leaving Georgie looking rather forlorn and abandoned.

'Here come the others.'

Everyone turned to watch as Ellen, Oliver and Seamus flew in from the far woods, carrying bundles. Gwen introduced them and invited everyone to sit around the fire, so they could talk. Duncan, still the least relaxed, decided to help Des with the grouse, leaving Oliver and Seamus to take the lead in any business with Humans. Lily reappeared, and she and Georgie took possession of the left boot, while Gwen brought water from the stream. Emily sat down next to Lisa. 'I can't believe this is happening!' she whispered. 'I promised my Gran before she died that I would try to bring understanding between Dragons and Humans. I'm so glad the Human is you!'

'We loved the books you and Megan gave us,' Alice added, sitting on her other side. 'We learned lots more about the lives of Humans, reading them.' Emily, trying to remember which books she and Megan had selected, wondered what strange ideas they would have believed.

Matthew began to feel a little awkward, excluded from these groups of old friends. As if she sensed this, Gwen motioned him over. 'Emily told me you are from Wales. I was born there too. And you and your friends saw the ceremony at my mother's death, she said?' Matthew nodded. 'It was fitting that you did. She always believed that we should try to befriend Humans. She and Duncan used to argue about it! Des is from Wales too – he knew Nan and Edward when he was growing up. Thank you for keeping us a secret, you and your friends who flew in the Dragons' Breath.'

'You weren't there, were you?' Matthew asked, puzzled. 'I thought I recognised Emily and Ollie, and Des of course, because of his painted wings, but the other two were not the same colour as you.'

'Emily sent me a picture through the Call,' Gwen explained. 'She and I both have the gift. I don't expect you to understand – lots of dragons don't either.'

'I think I know what you mean,' said Matthew. 'Some people have a gift like that – a *psychic* gift, we call it – but I haven't.'

'You have understanding, though,' Gwen smiled. 'I can feel it!'

As everyone was now settled, Seamus sent three huffed rings into the air – as if he was calling the meeting to order, Finn thought, amused. 'We all welcome you,' he said to the three visitors, 'and we would like you to answer some questions for us if you are willing.'

'Of course we are! What do you want to know?' Lisa asked.

'Were you all with the large group that spent time digging near the old castle?'

'I wasn't,' said Finn.

'Matt and I were, with a group from our University. Just for the last week. Others were here earlier, from another one. Nobody came up as far as this, at least not while we were there.'

'They didn't,' Des confirmed. 'As I told you earlier, you were watched.'

'We have never seen Humans here before. Why did you come?' It was Duncan, still suspicious.

'Humans from many years ago left traces of themselves hidden under the earth,' Lisa tried to explain. 'We were digging to find out about them. We knew they used to live there because of the stones of the old castle.' Emily, struck by an old memory, was looking amazed, and Seamus obviously knew what she was talking about.

'I have heard of this in Ireland,' he said. 'I told you that was their purpose, if you remember?' The young dragons nodded. 'Was that why you stayed by the castle, and nobody explored further up the Glen?' he added to Lisa.

'Yes, we were too busy. The dig was just three weeks. And when we went, we had to leave the place as we found it, as far as possible.'

'Tell me,' Des was listening while still attending to his cooking. 'Would we have been safe if we had showed ourselves to all of you? Emily thought we should try. She said you were the *right kind of Human*. I said it was too risky.'

Duncan huffed vigorously, obviously shocked by this revelation of how reckless his daughter could be, though her mother had smiled sympathetically.

Matthew and Lisa looked at each other thoughtfully. 'It's difficult to say,' Matthew said at last. 'We didn't know all of them well enough.'

'I think they were all the *right kind of Human*, though,' put in Lisa.

'But with so many there would be more chance that someone would let out the secret when we got back,' Matthew continued. 'We'd have been so excited! We're scientists, and you would have been a fantastic discovery. I'm still finding it difficult to believe, and I'd seen you once before. Just a glimpse, of course. I never got to know you, like Lisa and Finn. I think you were right, Des. The group was too big. It would have been too much of a risk.'

Des gave Emily a '*told you!*' look, which she pointedly ignored. Seamus nodded his agreement. 'I suppose you think we might be a risk too,' added Finn, 'but we've all kept your secret for years as we promised, so we've had lots of practice.'

Emily had been clutching the card she had found in one talon, and now she passed it to Lisa. 'Do you know this Human?' she enquired. 'Is he the right kind?'

'Phil's library card!' Lisa exclaimed. 'I wonder if he realised he'd dropped it.'

'He might not have missed it yet,' Matthew said.

'Is he the kind who would be safe to tell?'

Lisa and Matthew looked at each other again. 'He *might* be all right. Nice bloke, but a bit talkative!' said Matthew. 'Can we take it back for him?' Emily was obviously reluctant to lose her little souvenir but nodded her agreement.

'Why did you three come back to the glen after the rest had gone?' Oliver asked. The three looked at each other, thoughtfully.

'I just loved the place and wanted to see more of the wildlife,' Matthew said. 'But it was really Lisa. She believed that it might be the home of her long-lost dragon friends and persuaded Finn and me to come.'

'I just had a feeling you were here!' said Lisa simply. Gwen and Emily looked at each other and nodded. 'You heard the Call,' said Emily. 'I must have sent one without realising!'

'She does get these *feelings*,' Finn stated. 'We've often teased her about them.'

'Well perhaps you'll treat them with more respect from now on!' Lisa retorted, and Emily laughed. 'Probably not! Des doesn't always believe in mine.'

'So, are you saying that we would be wise to stay hidden and *not* attempt to contact a wider group of Humans?' Ellen asked. 'It seems to me that you know a good deal about us, from what we have seen of Human pictures and the stories Alice and Emily are so fond of. Though I must say, some of your ideas are very strange! How did we come to be creatures of legend?'

'I don't know,' said Emily. 'But everybody knows about dragons – all over the world!'

'It's a fascinating question,' Matthew added. 'I'm looking forward to working on it. In secret, of course!'

'Grouse is ready,' Des announced. 'There's some horrible pale bits for you three, and some properly crunchy ones for us. Make a start and I'll put the next lot on. We can carry on talking while we eat.'

Lisa, Matthew and Finn took the portions they were given rather gingerly. They were too hot to handle comfortably, so they laid them on the rock to cool, and then blew on them, which amused the dragons. But when they started eating, carefully nibbling the meat off the bones, they discovered it was delicious. They made a neat pile of the bones, noticing that the dragons crunched and swallowed theirs with a good deal of noise.

'So, Des tells me you're leaving our Glen today. Have we agreed that you won't be coming back?' asked Duncan when the noise of crunching had subsided.

'No!' Lily spluttered through a mouthful of grouse. 'They're coming back with Megan! I want to meet her properly!'

'Lily, I keep telling you it's not safe...' Duncan started, but Lily drowned his protest. She stamped her feet and there was fire in her indignant huff. 'That's not fair! Megan's MY Human. I want to see her again! If you won't let her come here, I'll go and find her by myself. I don't see why Emily and Tom can have *their* Human friends and I can't. It's not fair! You NEVER let me...'

'Shut up, Lily!' There was a combined weary chorus from Emily, Alice, Tom and Ollie, which sounded like a well-rehearsed response. All the other dragons started to laugh, except Georgie, who obviously wasn't sure whose side he was supposed to be on, and Seamus, who was trying not to interfere in a family matter. Lisa, Finn and Matthew grinned too; it was all so familiar!

'To get back to Dad's point,' Emily started the discussion up again, 'I think the answer's no! I don't see why they can't come again, and bring Megan – and Charlie too, if he wants to come. And anybody else they know they can trust. Just not too many, like Matt said.'

'What do you think, Seamus?' asked Oliver, trying to ignore Duncan's ominous huffs.

'I would agree with Emily,' Seamus said thoughtfully. 'In Ireland we have found great value in the friendship of Humans, and they have saved us more than once when we were threatened with discovery. They've introduced us to new food too. You're lucky here, having found such a deserted spot and a safe and roomy cave, but I believe a little Human contact could make your lives even better, and perhaps safer too.'

'And it looks to me as though we've found the right kind of Human,' Gwen said. Her voice was very quiet, but the way all the dragons turned to look at her told Lisa that her opinion counted for a lot in both families. There was a thoughtful and respectful silence, although Lily hissed 'Yesss!' under her breath and raised a clenched talon. Duncan still looked unconvinced.

'More grouse?' Des asked the three visitors, breaking the spell. 'Yours is done enough, I think.' There was a chorus of 'Yes please!'

'I'll hold it 'til it cools,' Ollie offered. 'You've got the wrong sort of talons.'

'Do you *really* have to go today?' Alice asked. Finn nodded with his mouth full. 'I wish we didn't, but we have to get back, especially if we want to come again,' he said. Lisa smiled to herself, pleased that the dragons, or perhaps the roast grouse, seemed to have cured Finn's negative mood. He was obviously enjoying this reunion as much as she was.

'It's quite a long hike to where we left the car,' Matthew explained. 'We'll need to spend another night in our tents, by the castle site. Then we have a long journey to the cities where we stay.'

Des and Duncan handed blackened grouse to the assembled dragons, and Ellen brought a pot of stream water to heat on the fire, Oliver helping the process along with a mighty huff. 'We only have dried nettles left for tea,' Emily apologised. 'Our stocks are rather low after the winter. Mint tea is our favourite, but we've none left. We've hardly any berries left either, or snails. I'm so sick of bulrush roots!'

'We miss your tatties when we're up here,' Ollie added. 'When we spent that bad winter in Angie's cellars we had them a lot, but you need to be near where Humans live to find them. They're great blackened in the fire.'

'We eat them like that too. When we next come we'll bring you a few, if we can fit them in our packs,' said Finn.

'Do you still live near Angie's Castle?' Tom asked.

'Yes, Finn and I do, but it's been knocked down now. There weren't any dragons left living in it, were there?'

'Three. Angie, Maggie and old Harold. We've never seen them again, so I don't know whether Humans caught them, or if they managed to escape. We've often wondered what became of them,' said Ellen, sadly.

'Lisa and I kept an eye on the newspapers to see if there were any reports of dragon sightings when the building was demolished, but there was nothing,' said Finn. 'They must have got away. We were a bit worried at the time.'

'Poor old Ange – no castle!' said Des. 'I wonder if she's found herself another one.'

'She could be a pain, but I don't like to think of her with no roof over her head,' Oliver agreed, crunching the last of the bones. 'Tasty grouse, Des! Thank you, Seamus – that was good hunting.'

'It was delicious! I wish we had more of our food left that we could share with you,' Lisa said. 'But I do have a few of these.' She pulled a handful of cereal bars out of her pockets. 'Would you like to try them? It's just oats and nuts and raisins, quite sweet.'

'We had some earlier,' said Alice. 'They're nice. Let the others taste them.'

'I wish I had more.' Lisa started to take wrappings off and Matthew emptied his pockets and passed the bars across. 'Oh great, Matt – I forgot you'd brought some too!' They were a considerable success with all the dragons, and the three of them made a mental note to bring a lot more next time. After they had tried a few sips of nettle tea, they resolved to bring an assortment of tea bags as well.

'Tell me something,' Des, his cooking over, sat down beside Matthew with his nettle tea. 'Those black things hanging round your neck. Emily called them *binoccies.* What are they for?'

'They let you see far-away things when you look through them,' Matthew explained, realising that it was no use demonstrating how dragons could use them, since their heads were the wrong shape. 'I use them to look at birds, mainly. Their real name is *binoculars*. How did you know what they were called?'

'Emily said. She and Alice have read so many Human books that they know all sorts of things. It can be quite useful.'

'Can you read too?'

'Nah! No point. I've got Emily.' Des grinned.

'We're often amazed at the things Humans know,' said Seamus. 'They may have some strange ideas about dragons, but some of their knowledge is very helpful. Our Humans have great interest in the land and its plants and creatures. Some dig deep in the ground to find out about the past, like you did. Some like exploring new places. It's amazing how well they can travel, for creatures with no wings.'

'Talking of travelling, I think we need to be getting back. It's going to take us a good while to walk to the dig site,' Finn jumped down from his place on the right boot.

'Oh Finn! Not yet!' Lisa emerged with difficulty from private talk with Emily and Alice. Des, his face contorted, was trying out the binoculars with one eye and then the other, shaking his head in a bemused fashion, and Matthew was trying not to laugh.

'We'll come down to the loch with you,' Ollie said. 'Have a swim, do some fishing.'

'Can you swim?' Tom enquired, secure in the knowledge that he could outswim any Human, even if the otters still beat him.

'Yes, but the loch will be too cold for us at this time of year,' said Finn.

'I'm really glad I wasn't born a Human!' Ollie declared. 'No wings, no talons and skin too thin for proper swimming.'

'And as for trying to light a fire…' Tom sniggered. 'Oh look! Here's Archie!' The large striped wildcat had appeared in their midst so stealthily that nobody had noticed. It glared round the assembled company, grabbed a grouse bone from the pile left by Finn and the others and leapt onto Ben's left boot to eat it.'

Lisa grabbed her phone from her back pocket. 'I *could* take a photo of Archie!' she said. 'Nobody needs to know he's tame!' Archie snarled loudly. 'Oops, sorry – 'course you're not tame. Great shots though.' The cat leapt down, grabbed another bone and disappeared round the gorse bush. Lisa managed another photo of his retreating back and splendid striped tail and showed Emily and Alice the tiny pictures. Seamus came to look too.

'One of my Humans has a machine like this, but much bigger,' he said. 'He wishes he could make a picture of us, but he knows how dangerous that would be.'

'It would be wonderful!' Lisa said. 'Can you imagine a photo of all of you. It's so tempting!'

'In full colour,' added Finn. 'Wildlife photo of the year!' At just the wrong moment, Duncan came out of the cave and heard the remark. 'How dare you!' he huffed, insulted.

'Calm down, Dad – it was a joke!' Tom explained, and Duncan allowed his huff to subside reluctantly. 'That wretched cat's in the cave again,' he complained, and flew down to the stream for a drink.

'Sorry!' said Finn, Tom and Emily simultaneously.

'If you really have to go, let's all go down to the loch to see you on your way,' said Alice, the peacemaker. 'We can walk through the woods. Lily and Georgie can come too.'

Duncan did not reappear, but the other parents came to bid their visitors farewell. 'Are you *sure* you would like us to come again?' Lisa asked. 'We could probably come in the summer, and we would love to bring Megan. But nobody else, we promise. And we won't tell anybody how to find this glen.'

'We trust you to keep your word,' Oliver assured them.

'Emily and I will try to send a Call if we have any news,' Gwen said to Lisa. 'I think you might hear a faint echo of it. I am so pleased you came. Don't worry about Duncan – we'll teach him to trust you too, I promise.' Lisa felt quite tearful as she said goodbye to Gwen. Des called

'See you down there. I'll fly after you. Need a word with Duncan,' and disappeared into the cave.

Tom had brought a smooth round stone from inside the cave, and as the six dragons and three humans made their way down the slope of the hill towards the wood, he, Ollie, Georgie and Lily passed it between them with flicks of their powerful tails. 'Looks as if you've Charlie to thank for that idea,' Finn remarked, attempting a kick as Georgie missed a pass and the stone veered towards him. 'Ow!' he added. 'I felt that even through my boot! Shows how tough their tails must be.'

'The big ball you gave us went soft and floppy ages ago,' Tom panted. 'And we brought small ones from the castle, but they got lost. We haven't been able to play decent tail-stane for years – the loch's not frozen right over since that bad winter.'

'I'll add tennis balls to the list of things to bring next time,' Finn promised.

'Tennis balls, tatties, tea bags and lots of cereal bars – we'll need a pack-pony,' Lisa said, delighted that a return visit seemed to be taken as a certainty. 'And Megan!' Lily called, overhearing.

At the edge of the wood, Lisa, Finn and Matthew turned and waved to the dragons on the hill, and then watched Oliver and Ellen fly up and head towards their own camp.

'Your parents are lovely!' Lisa said to Alice, 'And Gwen too. I wish Duncan wasn't so suspicious of us. I can understand why, I suppose.'

'We'll spend the next few weeks working on him,' Emily promised. 'Des has probably started already, though I suspect he stayed behind so he didn't have to *walk* to the loch.'

'He'll definitely join us there,' Alice added. 'He'll want to demonstrate his high diving!'

The tail-stane stone was abandoned at the edge of the wood, and the group wandered along the winding paths heading for the loch. 'Are other creatures afraid of you?' Matthew asked, noticing a squirrel flee up to the high branches of a tree and turn to chatter angrily at them.'

'Some are,' Ollie answered. 'Rabbits give us a wide berth, when they get the chance, and the hares keep clear! Most birds are OK, and the otters are very friendly, always have been. There's plenty of fish in the loch, so nobody goes hungry.'

'Winters can be hard,' said Emily. 'And we really miss Alice and the family when they go south. If only we could find another good cave, they could stay.'

The waters of the loch came in sight as the trees thinned, and they walked towards the little pile of rucksacks on the far shore. Ollie and Tom took to the air and dived into the loch as Des arrived, flying low to join Emily. 'Looks great,' said Finn, watching. 'Let's add wetsuits to the luggage next time. I bet it's chilly even in mid-summer. But imagine swimming with dragons!'

'And otters!' Emily added.

Lisa sat down on a convenient rock and eased off her left boot, wincing. 'What's up?' asked Finn.

'Blisters. Started yesterday, after I got my boot wet in the stream. I forgot to put new plasters on in all the excitement this morning. Ow!'

'I thought you were limping a bit,' said Matthew sympathetically. 'Is it bad?'

'They're bleeding. Can you fish the plasters out of the side pocket? It'll be all right if I pad it well.'

'I hope so!' said Finn. 'We've a fair walk ahead of us.'

'What is a *blister*?' Alice asked. Matthew explained while Finn helped Lisa to plaster up her heel, and the dragons shook their heads, baffled. 'Another good reason for being a dragon,' said Des, who had overheard Ollie's earlier remark. 'No need for boots and hide so thick you can jump a fire out without feeling it! Coming!' he called, hearing a shout from Ollie, hovering over the middle of the loch.

'Watch this!' said Alice. They all turned to look as Tom, Ollie and Des lined up in the air, then dived, snouts first, into the middle of the loch. It was perfectly coordinated, and the three gave a cheer and a hearty round of applause as the dragons surfaced, then swam across in arcing loops.

Lily and Georgie paddled out to meet them, and they all headed for the shore together.

''The otters go mad if they do that too often,' Emily said. 'Wattie's dad used to claim the fish died of fright when Des started it, years ago.'

'That needed a video!' Lisa said wistfully.

'A fitting finale!' Matthew declared. He was aware that Finn was itching to be on their way, especially as Lisa's blistered foot threatened to slow them down. She had eased her boot back on and the fresh plasters seemed to have lessened the pain.

'Yes, we must get started,' Finn said, shouldering his rucksack.

'Stand back!' Alice warned, as the five dragons waded out of the water and shook themselves violently, showering her and Emily as well as the three humans. It took the tension out of the leave-taking, and Lisa was able to smile. 'Goodbye, and thank you!' she said, then she and Finn said together, 'Stay safe!' in an echo of their farewell years before.

The three of them turned and walked steadily away along the edge of the loch without looking back, and the dragons watched, standing in a row on the bank. 'Poor things,' said Alice, 'trudging along so slowly. It'll take them ages to get back.'

'I suppose we couldn't try giving them a lift?' Ollie suggested to Des, but he shook his head. 'I might just manage

Lisa, but the boys would be too heavy. And she might be killed if she fell.' He saw that Lily and Georgie had splashed back into the loch and were out of earshot, and added, 'But it wouldn't take *us* long to reach that old castle where they're camping tonight. Let's sneak over and light them a fire – just the five of us. A surprise! Not a word to the others.'

Emily and Alice beamed at him as they spread their wings and prepared to fly home. Looking back once as they reached the far end of the loch, Lisa saw the multi-coloured group dwindle and disappear over the treetops and blinked back tears.

'Deer ahead,' said Matthew, trying to cheer her up as they crested the rise and began to pick their way down through the heather.

'No binoculars!' Finn warned. 'We need to push on if we're to get the tents pitched before dark. 'How's your foot feeling, Lisa?'

'Fine,' Lisa lied.

3

It was feeling a good deal worse by the time the castle mound came in sight, and their progress was also slowed by a rising wind blowing against them all the way. Ominous clouds were massing on the horizon. 'Looks like our luck might not last!' Finn remarked, pointing. 'Let's hope we can get the tents pitched before that hits. Can we go a bit faster?' Lisa sighed, and tried to mask the limp that was developing. 'You OK?' Matthew whispered, and was not convinced when she nodded.

Fixing her eyes on her feet so that she did not add a twisted ankle to her injury, she was not the first to spot signs of trouble ahead. Finn stopped so abruptly that the other two almost cannoned into him and pointed. A slight rise in the ground ahead hid the dig site, but a distinct spiral of smoke was rising above it. 'Oh no!' said Matthew. 'Not more campers! It can't be – we've seen no sign of anyone else.'

'Looks as if it is!' said Finn. 'I'll go on a bit until I can peer over and see what's there. You stay here. We might have to camp somewhere else instead. This *would* happen!' He sounded extremely irritated as he headed up the rise.

'Sit down for a minute,' Matthew said to Lisa. 'Can we do something about your foot while we've stopped? It's hurting quite a lot, isn't it?'

Lisa shook her head. 'I don't want to take my boot off. I'll only have to get it back on!' she said, trying to keep a sob from her voice. 'I'll sort it when we get there. Oh, Matt, it *can't* be other people in the glen! I couldn't bear it if our dragons were discovered and had to leave. We'll need to warn them, and how on earth can we manage that? Finn will never let us go back!' She squeezed her eyes shut, trying to keep tears at bay. Matthew crouched and put an arm round her.

'Let's wait and see,' he said, quietly. She rested her head on his shoulder and sniffed. 'Sorry!' she said, her voice muffled. He added his other arm and held her close, hoping that Finn would take his time. But in that respect, he was disappointed. Glancing up, he watched Finn reach the top, crouch, then crawl through the heather to peer down at the site. Then he leapt to his feet, turned and waved them over triumphantly. 'It's OK!' he yelled. Matthew pulled Lisa to her feet. 'Come on, obviously not as bad as we were thinking! Not far, then you can sort your blisters.' Lisa managed a watery smile of relief and followed him up the rise to where Finn was waiting, his expression guarded. Without a word he pointed down to the dig site, where six dragons – Seamus had joined them – were tending a sizeable bonfire. Emily spotted them on the skyline and waved. 'Aren't they wonderful!' said Lisa with a delighted smile, waving back.

'Fantastic fire!' said Finn, leading the way down. 'I was wondering how we'd manage that *and* tents before the rain hit. How on earth did they all get there without us seeing them?'

'I have a feeling they're pretty good at getting around unseen,' said Matthew. 'They know the area backwards. They're not exactly well camouflaged, though, are they?' Even under the rapidly darkening sky, the dragons' colours glowed in the firelight. Finn looked round, realising that Lisa was lagging behind, taking the slope carefully. 'Shall I push on and get started on the tents?' Matthew suggested. 'Her blister's pretty painful; that's what's slowing her down.'

Finn gave him a look that verged on the hostile. 'I'll go. You seem to be better at the supportive bit!' Without waiting for an answer, he plunged fast down the slope towards the dragons and the welcoming fire. Matthew waited for Lisa to catch up. 'Take it slowly,' he said, giving her a hand over a stony patch. 'Finn's gone ahead to start on the tents before the rain kicks in.'

'Finn's sulking,' she stated, staring at his retreating back.

'Yeah. I think he must have seen us back there. Sorry, Lisa. I didn't mean to cause trouble between the two of you.'

She changed the subject abruptly. 'I never thought they would fly round and meet us again. What a *fantastic* surprise. And a decent fire! I thought we were in for a cold night. Can't say I'm feeling hungry after all that grouse, but a hot drink would be wonderful. Or soup, perhaps.'

She had speeded up in her eagerness to reach them, almost forgetting the pain in her heel. Emily and Alice came to meet them as they neared the bottom of the hill. Lisa spread her arms wide. 'It's not fair, I want *wings*!' she proclaimed, ending almost in a run. 'You are wonderful! Whose idea was this?'

'Des thought of it,' Emily said proudly. 'We decided it should be just the five of us, but then we brought Seamus too. We managed to sneak off without telling Lily and the parents.'

'I'll go and help Finn with the tents,' said Matthew. 'Give me your pack and I'll put yours up too. Go and sit by the fire and take your boots off. Give them to me and I'll put them in your tent. I'm pretty sure I put an ankle support in my rucksack, in case of trouble,' he added. 'You can put that on tomorrow, over fresh plasters, before we set off.'

'Thanks Doctor Matthew!' Lisa called after him as he moved across to join Finn and sniggered at the rude hand gesture he made in response.

'I do like your friend Matt!' said Alice. 'We have a surprise for him. It should be along in a few minutes. No, I'm not telling you – it can be a surprise for you too.'

'I think you have a choice to make, Lisa!' said Emily mischievously, eyeing the two boys, erecting tents but not speaking to each other.

'I think she's made it!' said Alice, and the two dragons giggled happily at the expression on Lisa's face.

'Are *all* dragons mind-readers?' she asked.

'Gwen and Emily are,' said Alice. 'I'm not, usually – but that was easy!' Lisa sighed, and reflected that at least her companions weren't in earshot. A few minutes later they came across, having pitched the tents in a semi-circle, facing the fire, and Alice remarked, 'Oh good, just in time for Matt's surprise. Here she comes!' and pointed. A large and impressive brown and white bird flew low over the castle mound heading for them. There was a sizeable fish gripped in its talons.

'Must have visited our loch on the way,' Ollie said. 'Mum felt a bit guilty when you said you hadn't seen an osprey, Matt,' he added, 'so she asked one of them to fly over.' Matthew was speechless, and the dragons watched his expression of wonder as the magnificent bird flew close overhead, skirting the smoke, and headed back over the ridge, giving the dragons a yelping cry as it retreated. He and Lisa breathed a quiet 'Wow!' in unison as it disappeared, and Emily beamed her delight at their excitement. Even Finn looked impressed. 'Your Mum got it to do that!' he exclaimed. Ollie laughed. 'She probably promised we wouldn't fish in their loch for a day or two in return,' he said.

'If you come in the summer, we'll take you to our loch,' Alice promised Matthew, who was still too stunned to speak coherently. 'They have eggs just laid, so there'll be chicks in the nest. And the otter cubs will be out of the holt and playing in the big loch.'

'We MUST come back in the summer!' Lisa declared. 'If only we could let you know when we're coming! You might be off travelling.'

'Pity you can't Huff,' said Tom, and Emily explained what he meant. Matthew looked at Lisa, 'That must be what I saw from the castle. Those puffs of white in the distance,' he said.

'Hmm. Good thing it was only you!' Des said. 'Ellen was right about the dangers of Huff.'

'And was it you who flew over our camp in the middle of the night?' Lisa asked him. 'I heard heavy flapping wings in the mist. It frightened me to death!'

Des looked guilty. '*Might* have been,' he admitted. 'I did take a short cut one night, when I was carrying a load of grouse.' Ollie tutted loudly and Lisa sent triumphant glances at the boys. '*Wishful thinking*?' she mouthed.

'Water's hot if you want to make tea or something,' Des announced, changing the subject. 'Better make it before the rain starts. You haven't got long, by the look of that cloud.' Finn found some packets of soup, Lisa a remnant of cheese, and Matthew two apples. 'We've nothing left to share!' Lisa mourned.

'What are those?' Tom indicated the apples, but it was Ollie who answered. 'Humans' fruit. Grows on trees around where they live. You won't get any round here. Pity - they're good. Fill you up better than the likes of brambles and rowans.'

'Apples,' said Lisa. 'And we have pears and plums on our trees as well.' She found a last apple in the bottom of her pack and gave it to Tom, who bit it in half and handed the rest to Emily to try. They both nodded appreciatively. 'We'll add them to our list for the summer,' Lisa promised.

'Do you reckon we'll have time to go to Ireland before then?' Des looked across at Seamus, who nodded.

'I would like you to come if you can,' he said. 'I wanted to show you how Dragons and Humans can get along and help each other, but I think you have learnt that for yourselves today. You've been lucky in your first visitors. I expect you will want to bring others in time, and not just this Megan that Lily insists on meeting,' he added, addressing Lisa and the boys. 'Be careful and be sure you can trust the ones you bring.' They nodded.

'I'm glad to know you're bringing Megan,' Emily said. 'Lily's going to make such a fuss when she finds she can't come to Ireland! We can pretend she's got to stay to keep a look-out for you coming back with her.'

'When Lily is older, I would like to come back and escort her to Ireland, if her parents agree. My friends there won't believe I have found a pure gold dragon. And so brave and daring - she's like one of our Irish legends brought to life!'

Tom rolled his eyes and shook his head in horror. 'Tell her that and she'll be worse than ever!'

Heavy drops began to fall as Lisa and the boys finished their make-shift meal with hot chocolate - also approved by Emily and Alice and added to the list. 'Don't you want to head back to the cave before it gets going?' Matthew asked, but the dragons laughed. 'Only Humans fuss about rain,' Ollie said. 'We have decent waterproof scales!'

'But we should go, then you can crawl into your tents for shelter,' said Seamus. 'I will probably not be here when you return in summer, but I am honoured to have met you, and I wish you well.'

'We promise to stay safe,' Alice said, getting up.

'And you must promise to travel safely!' Emily added.

'Sorry we can't offer to fly you home,' said Des, offering High Fours. Ollie and Tom did the same, and Alice and Emily huffed gentle kisses. There was a chorus of 'good-byes' as six pairs of wings took to the darkening sky. The valley seemed suddenly very lonely. Lisa, blinking back tears, reached out her hands and both boys took them and moved closer. As they lost sight of the last dragon over the hill, the rain started in earnest, sizzling in the embers of the fire. Realising that Lisa had taken her boots off, the boys hoisted her between them and made a rush for the tents, pleased that her giggling protest took the tension out of the parting. All three were only too glad to burrow into sleeping bags and settle down for an early night. Lisa found the promised support bandage laid out on top of her rucksack, and blessed Doctor Matthew silently. 'I must think of a way to sort the boys out,' she thought, as she lay down, but was asleep before she had a chance.

The man concealed on the opposite hillside waited until the last gleam of torchlight from the three tents had been extinguished before stowing his binoculars in a battered knapsack and moving silently away through the rain.

LISA

1

Lisa, Finn and Matthew slept fitfully, despite their weariness. Intermittent drumming of heavy rain on the canvas combined with gusting wind made them fear for their tents, and damp seemed to seep into their sleeping bags. Just before dawn the rain stopped, but was replaced by heavy mist, which was little improvement. It was, however, silent, and they all fell more deeply asleep and woke a good deal later than Finn, at least, had intended. He crawled out first, shivering, and surveyed the sodden scene in front of him. A fire was out of the question, but he managed to light the Trangia for hot water before waking the others. They piled on as many layers as they could and emerged. Lisa sat in the opening of her tent, re-plastering her blister, and pulled on the support bandage with difficulty before easing on socks and boots.

'What food have we got left?' Finn asked. 'No point hoping for a full fry-up, obviously!'

'Tin of beans?' Matthew offered triumphantly. 'Now the water's boiled I'll heat them on the stove. Three spoons and eat them out of the pan.' He busied himself with this while Finn made tea and Lisa investigated her own pack. 'The last porridge pot – we can share that too. And a pack of apricots. Bit squashed. Thanks.' She took a gulp of tea. 'That's better! If we hadn't had all that grouse yesterday, we'd have run short of food. Need to bring more next time.'

'If I don't get the car back tonight, there won't *be* a next time! Let's get started on the tents while Matt does the beans. The sooner we get going the better. This mist's a pain, but at least we've a proper track from now on. How're the blisters?'

'Feel OK, I think. Matt's bandage is a help. Don't worry, I'll be fine. Ugh, these tents are sodden! Thank goodness we don't have to pitch them again.' The packing-up seemed worse than usual, but by the time the beans were ready it was finished. They brewed more tea, finished breakfast and felt able to start the last lap of their trek. Lisa carefully saved the last of her apricots for the hike ahead.

'I think the mist's clearing a bit,' Matthew said, optimistically but Finn grunted sceptically. 'At least there'll be no binocular-stops holding us up,' he retorted. 'Let's go.'

They found the track leading away from the site and set off towards the old hostel, walking in single file without talking. Lisa was almost glad of the mist and the silence. She wanted to relive the amazing experience of the previous day without distractions. She pictured the dragons emerging from their cave beneath that mysterious hill; perhaps they would see the mist and go back to bed! Or was hunting easier in the mist? She wondered if Emily and Des had stayed there, or whether they had flown on to their own cave in the gorge. She imagined the two of them together in their hidden retreat and smiled at the irony of Des the Traveller wanting to settle down and raise a family, while Emily was still enjoying the freedom to travel and explore. She hoped they would enjoy their Irish expedition and stay safe ....

Finn's phone suddenly buzzed, signalling the arrival of a text. Lisa woke from her reverie and they all stopped and stared at the mobile as if it had come from another universe. 'We've been climbing. Must have hit a signal spot,' said Matthew as Finn read the message and swore. 'Steve! He sent this yesterday. He wants the car first-thing tomorrow, earlier than he thought. Hell! We'd better hope there are no hold-ups. The sooner we can get to the car the better.' He attempted to send a return message, but the signal disappeared as abruptly as it had arrived. 'Can we pick up the pace?' he asked, waving his phone in the air, fruitlessly. The others nodded, fortified with water and one of Lisa's apricots.

Finn's new pace was so fast that Lisa, following him, occasionally lost sight of him in the mist and was glad that

Matthew was walking behind her. At least she wouldn't be left behind and alone in this grey wilderness. What a difference weather makes, she reflected. The sun, breeze and clear views of the previous days seemed like another world. At least her blister was not as painful as yesterday. As soon as she thought of it, it started hurting again! Matthew, watching her closely was aware that her stride had become uneven – not exactly a limp, but ominous. They were still some way from the hostel, and even further from the car. If only the mist would lift! They plodded on.

'Shouldn't we have reached the hostel by now?' Finn demanded, at their next water stop. 'We haven't hit on the wrong track, have we?' He was obviously getting more and more uptight since the text message had landed.

'I don't think there *is* another one and you can still see the wheel marks from the dig's jeep,' Matthew tried to be soothing. 'We've only been walking about two hours – I noted the time we left. I don't think it can be far now. OK to carry on?' he asked Lisa, who nodded. They set off in single file, as before, with Matthew still bringing up the rear and watching Lisa anxiously. Finn disappeared again.

It was actually only half an hour - though it seemed a good deal longer - when a triumphant shout from the invisible Finn echoed back to them. 'Here it is!' and they came to a wider and stonier section of track which sloped steeply downwards. Lisa remembered the laden jeep climbing painfully in a cloud of exhaust and grinned at Matthew as he came alongside. 'I was remembering the old dig truck only just making it up here!' she said.

'I'll never forget Sophie and the mud patch!' he said. 'I thought we'd seen the last of you both!' Finn loomed through the mist, catching their reminiscent chuckle, and then the walls of the hostel came into sight. Lisa sank thankfully onto the flat rock and wriggled her rucksack off. 'Water! Chocolate? No even better – Kendal Mint Cake! I'd forgotten this was still in the side pocket. I bet the dragons would have liked it. Add it to the list for next time.' She passed it round, but her determined cheerfulness did not fool Finn.

'I watched you come down that slope. Your blister's still bothering you, isn't it? Look, why don't you have a decent rest here. I'll push on up the track, fetch the car and bring it to pick you up. I can leave my pack with you. That'll speed me up.'

'Why don't I fetch the car?' Matthew offered. 'You stay here with Lisa.'

Finn was obviously tempted but shook his head reluctantly. 'Thanks, but better be me. The crate can be cranky about starting when it's been left in the cold.'

'So what if it doesn't and we get abandoned?' Lisa protested. 'At least if we stay together, there are two of us to push and get it going.'

'She's got a point,' said Matthew.

Finn thought for a minute. 'Compromise!' he decided. 'I'll push on ahead. You have as long a rest as you need, then follow me more slowly up the road. If there's no problem with the car, I'll drive it down to pick you up. I'd better take my pack.'

'No, leave it,' Matthew insisted. 'I can manage two. We've eaten most of the weight. Better take the car keys, though!' Finn hesitated, then nodded, collected the keys from an inside pocket and set off up the uneven road. He soon vanished into the mist, though they could hear the sound of his feet and the rattle of dislodged stones on the track for several more minutes. Lisa hunched herself up and shivered.

Matthew sat down beside her. 'Cold? Or worried?'

'Both.'

He resisted the temptation to put an arm round her and sighed heavily. 'My fault. I shouldn't have come. Though I wouldn't have missed it; it's been amazing! All of it, especially yesterday. But as soon as we get back to Glasgow I'll push off. You could stay on in Glasgow for a day or two. Finn'll be fine once I've gone, don't worry…' He tailed off as she turned to face him with the glint in her eye he had learned to be wary of.

'Don't you dare!' she said ferociously.

'Sorry?' He felt stunned.

'I *told* you! And I've told Finn! We had it out before we went to Uni. I *know* he's still hankering after us becoming *a couple*, but I don't feel the same way. I never will. He's my best friend, but that's *it*! I just wish he'd accept it. What I'm worried about now is losing his friendship – it would be like losing a brother. I couldn't bear it!' She bent her head, and he was afraid to break the silence between them. Then she swung round to face him again. 'But don't you see? *This* might force him to give up his dream and still stay friends.'

There was a pause.

'Is there a *this*?'

'Oh, I think so, Matthew Pritchard! Don't you?'

'I *hope* so, Lisa Elliot! I really do!' He watched the smile light her face as he pulled her into a hug and followed it with a kiss, feeling dizzy.

'That's settled then! Sealed with another kiss!' She demonstrated, gently, then got to her feet. 'I think we'd better plod slowly after Finn, before we get side-tracked. Come on!'

'Sure?'

'Of course I'm sure! I think I've been sure for a while. Certainly since yesterday!'

'I mean, is your blister fit to carry on up the track!'

'Blister? What blister? You've cured my blister, Doctor Matthew! Wow, I think you've made the mist clear too! I can see the hills appearing.' She picked up Finn's pack as well as her own.

'Give me that!' He made a grab for it, but she resisted. 'Let's swing it between us,' she said, offering him one of the straps. 'It'll be like holding hands. The mist *is* clearing – look! There are the mountain tops! Symbolic! Positively Shakespearean!'

He whisked the rucksack out of her grasp and took her hand instead. 'You are *mad*!' he declared as they set out to tackle the slope. 'And I thought I liked a quiet life! What *have* I done?'

'Nothing yet,' she sniggered. 'But there's plenty of time.'

2

Finn strode faster along the pot-holed road as soon as it levelled out, trying to blot out the picture of Lisa and Matthew laughing together as they descended the slope; concentrating on getting to the car, praying it would start, hoping the mist wouldn't last all the way to Glasgow. Fog and darkness, and not enough sleep.... or breakfast; he realised he was hungry and had nothing in his pockets. Dragons – he'd think about the dragons. That *had* been good. Fantastic! And Ollie and Tom had seemed as pleased to see him as Emily and Alice had been to see Lisa. The dragons had always been a bond between him and Lisa. Their secret. Perhaps it still would be. If only Matthew hadn't muscled in! Don't go there … He took a gulp from his water bottle and kept walking, head down, into the mist hardly noticing that it was thinning around him.

He had been on the road for about an hour when he spotted a Land Rover, moving towards him surprisingly fast, given its age and the state of the road. It bounced to a stop a little way ahead, the engine cut and an elderly man, clad in ancient brown waterproofs, a shapeless hat and boots caked in mud, climbed out and stood waiting, hands on hips. Finn walked towards him apprehensively, aware there was nothing else he could do.

'Ye'll be yin o' they youngsters campin' up the glen,' the man stated, without preamble. 'Ither two no', wi' ye? That your car doon yon?' He jerked a thumb over his shoulder as Finn approached.

'Yes,' Finn said breathlessly. 'Sorry if I wasn't supposed to park there. I thought it would be safe, off the road. The others are further back. My friend's limping a bit. Blisters. So I went on ahead to pick the car up. We're leaving today. We haven't done any damage up there, honestly – we were just hiking.' He ground to a halt, faced with the craggy and unresponsive face of the man in front of him.

'Aye, right. Ge' in. I'll gie ye a ride to pick 'em up.'

'Er – thanks. Are you sure?'

'Aye.' He climbed back into his jeep and Finn went round to the passenger door, opened it with difficulty and scrambled in.

'I'm glad the mist's clearing,' he said as they set off, trying to make conversation.

'Aye.'

'My name's Finn,' he tried again, peering ahead through the splattered windscreen.

'Ye can ca' me McPherson.'

'There they are!' he cried after a few minutes, pointing at the two figures on the road ahead in relief.

'Aye.' The man stopped where the track was slightly wider and made a five-point turn, driving into the muddy verge and missing the remains of fence posts and walling stones by millimetres. Finn jumped down as Matthew and Lisa came up. 'This guy picked me up. He's offered a lift to the car. He's not very talkative, but seems OK,' he added under his breath as he forced open the back door of the Land Rover and ushered them in. Lisa mouthed, 'The Factor!' at Matthew, who grimaced and nodded.

Finn climbed back into the jeep. 'Lisa and Matthew,' he said, back in the front seat. 'This is Mr McPherson.'

'This is very kind of you,' Lisa ventured.

'Aye.' The noise of the ancient vehicle bucketing over the rough track at speed made further conversation difficult, so they gave up, somewhat relieved. It did not seem long before they were swinging into the old quarry, where their car sat alone, with an abandoned air. McPherson pulled up with a jerk.

'Thanks a lot,' said Finn, opening his door and hoping for a quick get-away.

'Haud yer hurry! Yer pals are stuck back there whilst Ah get the door.' The old man climbed slowly out of the driving seat and prised open the rear door. Matthew and Lisa clambered out, dragging the three rucksacks, and looked helplessly at Finn, who shrugged. McPherson leaned back against his Land Rover, folded his arms and stared at each of them in turn. He turned his penetrating gaze on Lisa last.

'Ye were yin o' the diggers at the broch a while back, aye?'

'I was too,' Matthew cut in hastily.

'Aye,' he transferred the gaze, 'and ye'll be one for spying on the birds, if yer field-glasses gie me a clue. Was that why ye came back to trespass up yon glen, aye?'

'Yes,' said Lisa, with what she hoped was a winning smile. 'We loved our time at the dig and we decided to explore a bit further. Honestly, we've done no harm. We did camp, but we haven't left any litter or anything, honestly. And we were very careful with our fires.'

'And I left the car here. I didn't think it would be in anybody's way off the road,' added Finn. McPherson did not appear to be listening to them.

'Sae tell me - what creatures huv ye spotted up there?' he shot at Matthew.

'Er - there was a pair of black-throated divers on the loch up the glen. I've never seen them before. And we saw an osprey flying past. Ravens and a pair of eagles. And lots of smaller birds, of course, a dipper, coots....' He tailed off.

'And there were two otters on the loch,' Lisa added.

'Aye, right. And ye saw naught else ye micht want to tell yer friends aboot when ye get hame?'

'Well, those were pretty good. Worth the trip!' Matthew hedged.

'Aye mebbe.' He paused, thoughtfully. 'So, it wasna' the three of ye sittin' roond the fire by the broch yesternicht, wi six strange coloured beasties?' he demanded, casting a stern glance at each horrified face in turn. They were silent, not knowing what to say. 'I huv the field-glasses tae, y'ken, and I watched ye a' fer near an hour afore the rain came on.'

There was a shocked silence. Then Lisa whispered. 'Oh no! We've given them away! Please, please Mr McPherson, you mustn't tell anyone. They're not doing any harm up there. *Please* keep them a secret!'

A slow smile transformed the old man's face, creasing it into wrinkles. 'Aye weel, lassie, Ah've been keepin' thae beasties a secret fer seven years and more. What ah want tae ken is, will youse be daein' the same?' He pointed an admonishing finger at each in turn.

The three looked at each other, shock, wonder and relief mingled. Then Finn took a deep breath. 'We've been keeping their secret for years too.'

McPherson looked puzzled. 'Is that richt? How so?'

'Six years ago, that very bad winter, they were hiding in an old ruin near our home in Northumberland. We discovered them by chance, and we promised that we'd tell nobody about them. We know quite well what might happen to them if the wrong people found out.'

'Aye, I mind that bad year. So the canny beasties flew south fer the winter! An me thinkin' they'd perished in the cauld! Ah wiz glad tae see them back in the thaw. Ye must ha' bin bairns back then. Were ye no' scairt o' them?'

'They were a bit scary, but the young ones were friendly,' Lisa said. 'They told us all about....'

'Dinnae tell me ony mair,' the old man interrupted, holding up a warning hand. 'Ah ken fine they're bidin' up the glen, and ah ken they tak ma grouse – the're welcome tae tak them. Better thae that need the food than the rich fools that come fer the shoot'n.' He spat contemptuously. 'Frae time te time ah catch a wee glimpse o' yin o' them flyin' o'er the hills. 'Specially that big green yin wi' stripy wings…'

'That's Des,' Lisa broke in.

'Ye've gi'ed them names, Ah dinna doot!' the old man smiled at her. 'Ah dinna want te ken ony mair! Dinnae fash, lassie! There's naeb'dy else treks up that glen. Folk used to tell it was haunted by the ghosts o' them killed in the battle of the broch i' the auld days. Ma great-granny telt of giants that dwelt there, but she was aye one for selkies and kelpies and giants and such. Yon foreign laird that owns the land doesna' care nor visit much. Ah'm the Factor in charge, so yer dragons are safe, as lang as they're canny.' He gazed keenly at all three in turn. 'If ye'll keep their secret safe, ye're welcome to come back. Just youse, mind! And if ye let me ken y're coming, Ah'll no' fret if Ah see a strange car left hereaboots.'

'We *were* thinking we'd like to come back in the summer,' Lisa said tentatively. 'But how can we let you know?'

McPherson gave a roar of laughter. 'Ah'm no' yin o' yer dragons, lassie - ye can gie me a ring! No' on yin o' yer mobiles, 'cos they dinnae work roond here, but Ah've a phone in ma hoose.' He chuckled again, and slowly recited the number for Matthew to enter into his phone.

'We should get going,' Finn said, as Matthew put his phone away. 'Thanks a lot, Mr McPherson.'

'Ye dinnae need the mister, laddie! I'll be seeing youse again. I'll keep an eye out fer yon dragons fer ye.'

'Thanks a lot! You gave us quite a fright there.' Matthew held out a hand for McPherson to shake before he turned to help Finn load the car.

'Would you do something for me – well, for the dragons really?' Lisa ventured, holding out her own hand.

'Aye lassie, whit's that?'

'They're a bit short of food after the winter. Could you leave a bag of tatties for them at the broch, without them seeing? They roast them in the fire. They say they're sick of bulrush roots. They call us *the right kind of Human* and I think you are too. Please?'

The old man had kept hold of her hand. 'Lassie, I'd no' find it in me to say no tae one as bonny! Ah c'n see how ye charmed yon beasties. Ah'll dae that. Awa' ye go noo! Yer laddies're waitin' fer ye.'

'Thank you *so* much!' She gave him a beaming smile as she climbed into the front seat of the car. It took three tries, but to Finn's relief the engine started at last, and Lisa leaned out of the open window and waved as they slowly swung round and out onto the road home.

3

'Is anyone else as hungry as me?' Finn enquired, breaking the silence as he steered the car carefully round the ruts and holes in the road. They were still feeling shell-shocked after their encounter with McPherson, and not inclined to chatter.

'Me!' a heartfelt exclamation from the back seat.

'And me! We've got time to stop at that nice eatery, haven't we?' Lisa turned to Finn. 'They did hot stuff as well as cakes and things. I really feel like fish and chips, but we might have rather a long hunt for that.'

'And a long wait – they're not usually open until later. I can't think how Steve's tyres are surviving this!'

'There's the first set of iron gates,' Matthew observed a while later. 'Not far to the main road.'

'Good. It didn't seem to take nearly as long coming in.'

'Perhaps we'll never get out. Perhaps it's a magic road, leading to the haunted glen with its ghosts and giants, and it doesn't let you escape. I liked the sound of Mcwhatsit's Great Granny, didn't you? I bet she'd have loved the dragons.'

'She sounded a bit like you!'

'That weird bald-headed hill gave rise to a local giant legend, I expect,' Matthew observed. 'And I'm sure all ruined brochs are said to be haunted. Welsh castles usually are too.'

'No, it's all true! Stop being a rational scientist!'

'Sorry! I think that line of trees ahead marks the main road, Finn.'

'Good. At least the mist's cleared.' Finn sounded slightly more cheerful. 'We should get a fair stretch of the way home before dark. The old guy's lift saved us quite a bit.' As the turning came up and he swung onto smooth tarmac he gave a sigh of relief. 'Right, stay awake until we get to the café. Don't let me shoot past it. I just hope it's open!'

It was, and the hot dish of the day proved to be an excellent veggie lasagne, which they devoured hungrily, finishing with brownies and coffee. 'That's woken me up nicely,' Matthew said. 'I was beginning to doze off back there. I'll drive for a stretch, if you two want to snooze in the back. I shouldn't need a navigator, heading home.'

'OK, thanks, I might just do that!' said Finn. 'Until we get near Glasgow, anyway. But Lisa had better sit in the front and keep you awake.'

'OK. I can remind him where the indicator is.'

'Cheek!' said Matthew. 'Not being a driver yourself, you won't realise the challenge of a strange car.'

'She did *try* passing her driving test before going to Uni,' Finn remarked, 'but failed!'

Lisa kicked him under the table. 'You rat, Finn! Giving me away! OK, Matt, I admit it. I *did* fail. He was a *horrible* examiner; old and cranky and probably prejudiced against women drivers.'

'Not charm-able, like old McPherson, then?' Matthew insinuated. Finn grinned, and Lisa rose with dignity, and fixed them both with a steely glare. 'I'm going to the loo, and if I find you sharing any more of my darkest secrets, Finn...' She departed, nose in the air, inwardly delighted; her boys were ganging up on her – that was an improvement! Left at the table, they shared eye-rolls, head-shakes and rueful grins.

'I'll settle the bill,' Matthew said, getting up. 'I presume you'll need to fill the car up before handing it over. There's the bottle of Scotch for Steve too. We can work out who owes what when we get back.' He went to the bar to pay, adding some of Lisa's favourite chocolate, and mints to keep himself awake.

Back on the road, Finn soon fell asleep in the back and Lisa padded the side window with her fleece and leaned her head against it. 'Go to sleep if you want to,' Matthew said quietly, 'I won't fall asleep at the wheel, honestly. I had a good shot of caffeine.'

'I don't want to. I just want to sit here and think about our dragons. It feels a bit like a dream, now. We *must* come back in the summer.'

'Yes, now that we have the old guy's permission! I don't think Des and Co have any idea that he knows about them. Des would be mortified – he thinks *he's* the glen's secret spy!'

'D'you think we should tell them?'

'You decide! You know them best.'

'Hmm. Need to think about that one.'

'I wonder if he'll leave their tatties.'

'Of course he will! He promised! I'd love to see their faces when they find them.'

'You magicked that promise out of him. You have fatal charm, Lisa Elliot – me, Finn, old McPherson, the guys at the dig. Even Dave Andrews, if Sophie's to be believed; though that might be more your neat way with a trowel. Gwen and Emily think you're psychic; are you?'

'Of course! I can weave spells, read thoughts, magic a promise and speak with dragons. I'm a witch!'

'Dangerous woman! Distracting anyway. I ought to concentrate on driving. You dream up a story to explain how you happen to have Phil's library pass.'

'We must keep our dragons a deadly secret when we get back, you know,' she said, suddenly serious. 'Never let *any* hint slip out. Especially not to the diggers, who know where the glen is. Thinking of Phil and how he can blether after a drink or two made me realise the danger.'

'I know! I'll be very careful. Deadly secret. Ours!' He glanced sideways at her. 'Do you wish you were back there?'

'Not really. It's their place. We're going back to ours. Are you going to keep me – I mean *us* - a deadly secret when we get back?'

'No way!' he said, firmly. 'There's a queue for *your* favours. I could probably manage to take Phil on in a duel, but I'm not sure about Sandy. He's a hefty bloke! Then there's Paul. He admitted he fancied you, more or less, on that last evening outside Hall.'

'You are having me on!' she had turned to face him, and he kept his eyes on the road ahead with difficulty.

'Not! You wait 'til we get back. You'll see.'

'Then you'll have to protect me from their unwelcome attentions, my Welsh Knight-in-shining-armour! It can be your project for the term, along with coming out top in the end of year exams. Should be easy enough to manage both, shouldn't it?'

'Depends on the level of distraction! Give me some chocolate and go back to your dragon dreams. I really do need to concentrate – it's getting dark.'

'I'll just check you know where the headlights are. Well done! Here's the choc, then.' She fed him a piece then rested on her fleece and closed her eyes. 'Hmmm, nice dreams…' she remarked. Matthew peered into the gloom ahead, a smile on his face. He could hardly believe the change a few hours had made in the prospects for the term ahead.

4

It was mid-evening when they finally pulled up outside Finn's flat. He had not woken up until they neared the outskirts of Glasgow, but then had directed Matthew to a garage with shop attached, where he filled the car and Lisa purchased a bottle of Steve's favourite expensive malt. The three bills, including the lunch, were close enough to make complicated settling-up unnecessary, they decided and Finn, knowing his way around the city, took over the driving, to Matthew's relief.

Texts to the flat had yielded the information that all of Finn's flatmates, including partners, had returned, and Lisa and Matthew decided to catch an evening train to Edinburgh rather than reuse their damp sleeping-bags. 'If you dash up to collect the stuff you left, I'll stay double-parked outside and run you round to the station,' Finn said as they neared his street. 'If I'm not there when you come down, I'll be driving round the block.'

'I've only got what's in the car,' said Lisa.

'What about all your stuff for the term?' Matthew asked.

'Oh, Dad was driving round Edinburgh on his way north for work a couple of days ago. I persuaded him to drop all my stuff at Ewing for me. It wasn't much of a detour. He said he didn't mind.'

'Some people have all the luck!' said Matthew admiringly.

'You'll find she's very good at persuading people to do inconvenient things,' Finn remarked. 'Famous for it.'

'I had noticed,' Matthew admitted, 'treks, dragons, tatties, luggage…' Lisa, delivering a punch to Finn, aimed one for him as well.

Finn was right – his street was close-parked. He handed over his key and left the engine running on a double yellow line, keeping an eye out for cruising police cars, while Lisa and Matthew dashed in for his holdall, computer bag and guitar, left packed and ready in the hall. 'Good thing you're so organised,' Lisa said as they hurried back down the stairs and made for the car.

Finn pulled up on the station forecourt and helped them unload. Lisa dropped her rucksack to give him a long and heart-felt hug. 'Thank you SO much, Finn!' she said. 'It was a WONDERFUL trip. Facetime next weekend? I'll message as usual and we can fix the time. And come over for a weekend mid-term, so we can plot the summer expedition.'

Finn pulled away to give her a searching look. 'Yeah?' he said. 'Sure?'

''Course I'm sure, bro!' She planted a kiss on his cheek, then rubbed a hand on it. 'You know, that stubbly look rather suits you. I'd keep it!'

'If you say so, sis – you're the boss!' He flicked a glance at Matthew over Lisa's head, and caught a sympathetic smile. 'Cheers, Matt! Thanks for the driving,' he said. 'And best of luck!'

'You reckon I'll need it?'

'Oh yes! Nae doot aboot it, as McPherson might say.'

'You're a rotten pair,' Lisa complained. 'I can't think why I like you both!'

She and Matthew heaved the luggage between them into the station and turned to wave, but Finn had already started the car and was driving away. 'Poor guy!' said Matthew quietly.

'He'll get over it,' said Lisa, trying to sound confident, but aware of a lump in her throat. 'I'm sure there's a nice girl for him at his uni. I just hope I'll be able to get on with her. She has to be the *right kind of Human!*'

'Trust Finn. He has good taste.'

She grinned more cheerfully. 'Train in ten minutes, and it's there already. Let's get tickets and grab a seat.'

They stowed the luggage into an almost empty compartment and settled into seats, hoping the quiet would last. 'Good job it stops at Waverley,' Lisa remarked yawning. 'We can both go to sleep in safety, knowing we won't end up in Newcastle. *You* must be tired, after all that driving.' She leaned against him comfortably. 'You know what I said about Finn's unshaven look – it suits you too. I said so before, remember?'

'No!' he said firmly. 'You might be the boss, but that's a red line. I hate it – it's so itchy. Drives me mad!'

'Sure?' she sighed. 'Pity; but if you insist I suppose I'll have to give in! For now. I hope there won't be too many of those,' she added suspiciously.

'Red lines? Don't think so.'

'Good.'

'There is a pinkish one…' he ventured. She looked up quizzically. 'You know I said I didn't want to keep it a secret?'

'Ye-es? Because of the danger of duels with rival suitors? Not that I believe in them!'

'But we don't have to go around like Cassie and Whoever all the time, do we? I'm not sure I could cope with a public wrap-around relationship.'

She gave a delighted giggle. 'That's a lovely way of putting it! No, I agree. I can live without a wrap-around one.'

'Good. Any red lines from you?'

'Not yet! I'm still thinking. There's not minding about Finn and me, obviously.'

'Obviously.' She glanced up at his expression, but there was no trace of sarcasm. 'Yes, obviously! You're best mates! I have some at home too – girls as well.'

She smiled. 'You'll need to teach me some Welsh before I get to meet them.'

The train gave warning bleeps, closed its doors and started to move. He put his arm round her and she snuggled against his shoulder as it picked up speed. The lights of the city made a flashing kaleidoscope. 'Our secret glen seems a million miles away. Did it really happen?' Lisa murmured.

'Seems a bit dream-like doesn't it? But we'll be back in the summer.'

'What if Finn can't get the car?'

'I'll find another way, I promise.'

'Good! Emily and Alice will be really pleased about us.'

'D'you mean to say you've been discussing me with *dragons*!' he said in mock outrage.

'I didn't need to. They knew. Alice said it was obvious, even though it's Emily that's the psychic one. I wonder if she could hear if I gave her a Call.'

'No doubt you'll both give it a go. Let me know if you get through.'

She giggled, heaved a deep sigh and closed her eyes. 'I've just had a great idea for the term!' she announced.

'Oh no! What's it this time?'

'Something that will please the Welshman in you and send our conductor into ecstasies. You can join the choir!' Opening her eyes a fraction, she registered a smile and a nod of agreement, or possibly relief, and decided to leave the idea of busking, for a little while longer...

Clearing the city outskirts, the train picked up speed and headed through the dark for Edinburgh.

Author's Note

Loyal readers of the Dragon Tales Chronicles will recognise most of the main characters in this book, both Human and Dragon, and I hope they will be happy with the way their favourites have grown up and their lives have changed since that series was completed two years ago. The Glen itself remains the unspoiled wilderness of the earlier books.

New readers might like to know that the 'back story' of Lisa, Finn and Matthew, along with many past experiences of members of the Dragon Clan alluded to in this book, can be found in *Dragons in Snow* and *The Dragons' Call* – Books V and VI of the series.

Copies of these books can be ordered from:
www.practicalinspiration.com

Acknowledgements

As always, my five grandchildren, Phoebe, Elise, David, Sam and Megan have provided inspiration for a good deal of this story, as they, like the characters, grow up. I'm sure they will recognise something of themselves in the Humans and the Dragons in this one. So, thanks to them for sharing their love of hiking and camping and sport and music and wildlife.

Thanks especially to Elise, my Editor in Chief, principal critic in the writing of credible teenage dialogue and technical references, design consultant and strummer of a ukulele. And to Kate, who gave valuable criticism of the first draft and encouragement generally, and, with Roddy, reminded me of details of their own student life in Edinburgh.

Thanks to Martin for introducing me to a Trangia; Gordon, for checking and correcting McPherson's Scots dialect; and Peter, for proof-reading and patience with my preoccupation while writing this.

Special thanks to Gill for recommending David as a graphic artist – and of course to David!

And *very* special thanks to Alison and Michelle at Practical Inspiration Publishing, for fitting valuable advice to this elderly, tech-phobic author into their frenetic work schedule.